# Look what people are saying about Jill Shalvis...

"Riveting suspense laced with humor and heart is her hallmark and Jill Shalvis always delivers."
—USA TODAY bestselling author Donna Kauffman

"Romance does not get better than a Jill Shalvis story."
—romancejunkies.com

"Shalvis firmly establishes herself as a writer of fast-paced, edgy but realistic romantic suspense, with believable and likable supporting characters and fiercely evocative descriptive passages."
—Booklist

"For those of you who haven't read Jill Shalvis, you are really missing out."
—In The Library Reviews

"Danger, adrenaline and firefighting heat up the mix in Jill Shalvis's blistering new novel."
—Romantic Times BOOKreviews on White Heat

"Jill Shalvis displays the soul of a poet with her deft pen, creating a powerful atmosphere."
—WordWeaving

"Jill Shalvis is a breath of fresh air on a hot, humid night."
—thereadersconnection.com

# Blaze™

Dear Reader,

When I start to write a romance novel, it's usually all about the fantasy. Girl meets Hot Guy. Hot Guy falls hard. You know the drill. But this book is a little different. You see, this time, reality intruded—in my life, and in my writing.

Several members of my immediate family were evacuated in the tragic San Diego fires this past fall, about the same time I was finishing up this book. And suddenly this miniseries, AMERICAN HEROES: THE FIREFIGHTERS, became more than a romantic fantasy for me. Sure, I wanted to give readers a sexy tale that would keep them enthralled right through to the end. That's always my goal. But I also wanted to honor these amazing, strong firefighters who put their lives on the line for real, every day.

I hope I did them justice.

Best wishes and happy reading!

*Jill Shalvis*

P.S. If you still need a firefighter fix, you don't have long to wait—the 2008 Harlequin Blaze Christmas anthology, *Heating up the Holidays*, will hit the shelves in December. And if you missed it, be sure to check out my connecting book, *Flashpoint*, available last month.

# JILL SHALVIS
## Flashback

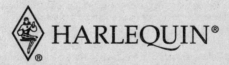

# HARLEQUIN®

TORONTO • NEW YORK • LONDON
AMSTERDAM • PARIS • SYDNEY • HAMBURG
STOCKHOLM • ATHENS • TOKYO • MILAN • MADRID
PRAGUE • WARSAW • BUDAPEST • AUCKLAND

ISBN-13: 978-0-373-79420-1
ISBN-10:    0-373-79420-7

FLASHBACK

www.eHarlequin.com

**Printed in U.S.A.**

## ABOUT THE AUTHOR

*USA TODAY* bestselling author Jill Shalvis is happily
writing her next book from her neck of the Sierras.
You can find her romances wherever books are sold,
or visit her on the Web at www.jillshalvis.com/blog.

### Books by Jill Shalvis

Don't miss any of our special offers. Write to us at the
following address for information on our newest releases.

Harlequin Reader Service
U.S.: 3010 Walden Ave., P.O. Box 1325, Buffalo, NY 14269
Canadian: P.O. Box 609, Fort Erie, Ont. L2A 5X3

# 1

THE FIRE BELL RANG for the fourth time since midnight, interrupting Aidan Donnelly in the middle of a great dream in which he was having some fairly creative, acrobatic sex with a gorgeous blonde. The last thing he wanted was to be shaken awake, but apparently sex, imaginary or otherwise, wasn't on his card for the evening.

He was on the last few hours of a double shift from hell. The loudspeaker mounted in one corner of the bunk room was going off, telling him and his crew that they would not be going home in one short hour after all, but back into the field on yet another emergency call.

Putting the blonde back where she belonged, in the file in his brain labeled Hot Erotic Fantasy, Aidan got up to the tune of a bunch of moans and groans from his crew.

So close. He'd been so close to three desperately needed days off....

Across the room Eddie kicked aside the latest issue of *Time,* which had an entire company of firefighters on the cover. "A lot of good being the sexiest occupation does us," the firefighter grumbled, "when we're too exhausted to take advantage of it."

"Some of us don't need beauty sleep." This from Sam, Eddie's partner. "Like, say, Mr. 2008 here." He slid a look Aidan's way, but Aidan found himself too tired to rise to the bait.

Through no fault of his own, he'd been named Santa Rey's hottest firefighter for 2008. This dubious honor came along with another—being put on the cover of Santa Rey's annual firefighter's calendar. "I told you, I didn't submit my name."

Eddie grinned in the middle of dressing. "No, we did, Mr. 2008."

Aidan gave him a shove, and Eddie fell back to the mattress, snorting out a laugh as he staggered upright again and grabbed his boots. "Yeah, like being that pretty is a hindrance."

"I am not pretty."

No one answered him in words as they pulled on their gear, but several made kissy noises as they headed toward their rigs. Still groggy, and definitely out of sorts, Aidan took the shotgun position next to Ty, his temporary partner, on loan from a neighboring firehouse, since his usual partner Zach was still off on medical leave.

Eddie and Sam grabbed their seats, as well as Cristina and Aaron, another on-loan firefighter, and they were all off into the dark night—or more accurately, the dark predawn morning—following the ambulance, which had pulled out first. The air was thick with dew, and salty from the ocean only one block over. For now the temperature was cool enough, but by midday the California August heat would be in full bloom, and they'd all be dying. Aidan got on the radio to talk to dispatch. "It's an explosion," he told the others grimly.

"Where?" Ty asked.

"The docks." Which could be anywhere from the shipping area, to the houseboats filled with year-round residents. "Only one boat's on fire, but several others are threatened by the flames, with no word on what caused the explosion."

Behind him, Eddie swore softly, and Aidan's thoughts echoed the sentiment. Explosions were trickier than a regular fire, and far more unpredictable.

"Are they calling for backup?" Sam asked.

They needed it. Firehouse Thirty-Four was sorely overworked and dangerously exhausted going into the high fire season. They'd had a rough month. Aidan's partner and best friend Zach had been injured after digging into the mysterious arsons that had plagued Santa Rey. Mysterious arsons that were now linked to one of their own.

Blake Stafford.

Just the thought brought a stab of fresh pain to Aidan's chest. Now Zach was off duty and Blake was dead, leaving them all devastated.

Cristina was especially devastated, and with good reason. She'd been Blake's partner, and the closest to him. She'd suffered like hell over his loss, and also over the arsons he'd been accused of committing.

She blamed herself, Aidan knew, which was ridiculous. She couldn't have stopped Blake.

As it turned out, none of them could have stopped him.

Aidan considered himself pretty damn tough and just about one-hundred-percent impenetrable, but losing Blake had been heart-wrenching. He missed him, and hated what he'd been accused of. He didn't want to believe Blake was dead, and he sure as hell didn't want to believe Blake guilty of arson, and the resulting death of a small boy—none of them did, but the evidence was there. He could hardly even stand thinking about it—classic denial, Aidan knew, but it was working for him. "Dispatch's sending rigs from Stations Thirty-Three and Thirty-Five."

No one said anything to this, but they were all thinking the same thing—it'd take those stations at least ten extra minutes to get on scene from their locations—and the sense of dread only increased as they pulled up to the docks.

Turned out that the fire wasn't at the shipping docks, but where the smaller, privately owned boats were moored at four long docks, each with ten bays. Possibly forty boats in total, many of them occupied.

Chaos reined in the predawn. Their senior officer was usually first on scene, setting up a command center, but he was coming from another fire and was five minutes behind them. The sky was still dark, with no moon, and the visibility wasn't helped by the thick plumes of black smoke choking the air out of their lungs. Flames leaped fifty feet into the air, coming from a boat halfway down the second of the four docks. Aidan took a quick count, and his stomach tightened with fear. There were boats on either side of the flaming vessel, and more on the opposite side of the dock.

Not good.

As they accessed their equipment and laid out lines, three police squad cars tore into the lot, followed by the command squad, all of whom leaped to work evacuating the surrounding docks. Aidan and company needed to contain the flames, but the explosion burned outrageously hot. He could feel that mind-numbing heat from a hundred feet back. With the chief now on scene, barking orders through their radios, Aidan and the others moved with their hoses, their objective to keep the flames from spreading to any of the other boats. They were halfway there when it came.

A sharp, terrified scream.

The sound raised the hair on the back of Aidan's neck, and he dropped everything to run toward the burning boat, Ty right behind him.

The scream came again, clearly female, and Aidan sped up. No one knew better than a firefighter what it was like to be surrounded by flames, to have them lick at you, toy with you. It was sheer, horrifying terror.

They had to get to her first.

Behind them came Sam, Eddie, Cristina and Aaron, directing water on the flames to clear Aidan and Ty's path down the dock toward the boat. Twenty feet, then ten, and that's when he saw her. A woman standing on the deck of the burning boat, wobbling, the flames at her back.

"Jump!" he yelled, wondering why she didn't just make the short leap to the dock—she could have made a run for safety. "*Jump*—"

Another explosion rocked them all. Aidan skidded to a halt, spinning away and crouching down as debris flew up into the air to match the intensifying flames. The chief was shouting into the radio, demanding a head count. Aidan lifted his head and checked in as he took in the sights. The boat was still there. With his heart in his throat, he searched for a visual on the woman—

*There.* In the same spot she'd been before, still on the deck but on the floor now, holding her head. *Goddammit.* He got to his feet, took a few running steps, and dove onto the boat.

She nearly jumped out of her skin when he landed next to her. "It's okay." He dropped to his knees at her side to try to get a good look and see how badly she was injured, but the smoke had choked out any light from the docks and she was nothing but a slight shadow. A slight shadow who was hunched over and coughing uncontrollably.

"The boat," she managed. "It k-keeps b-blowing up—"

"Can you stand?"

"Yes. I—" She let out a sound that tugged at his memory, but he pushed that aside when she nodded. She got up with his help, twisting away from him to stare up at the flames shooting up the mast and sails. "Ohmigod…"

He pulled her closer to his side, intending to jump with her to the dock and the hell off this inferno, but several things hit him at once.

The name of the boat painted across the outside of the cabin, flickering in and out of view between the flames. *Blake's Girl.*

No. It couldn't be. Then came something of far more immediate concern—the rumbling and shuddering of the deck beneath their feet. "We have to move."

"No. No, please," she gasped. "You have to save the boat."

"Us first." He couldn't have put together a more coherent sentence because of all that was going through his head. *Blake's Girl...*

Blake's boat. God, he'd all but forgotten that Blake had owned a boat.

Then there was the woman in his arms, facing away from him, but invoking that niggling sense of familiarity. There was something about her wild blond curls, about the sound of her voice—

The warning signals in his brain peaked at once. In just the past thirty seconds, the flames had doubled in strength and heat. The deck beneath their feet trembled and quivered with latent simmering violence.

They were going to blow sky high. Whipping toward the dock he got another nasty surprise—the flames had covered their safe exit.

On the other side of those monstrous flames stood Ty, Eddie and Sam, hoses in hand, battling the fire from their angle, which wasn't going to help Aidan and his victim in time. Cristina was there, too, with Aaron, and even in the dark he sensed their urgency, their utter determination to keep him safe.

They'd so recently lost one of their own; there was no way they were going to let it happen again.

"Ohmigod," the woman at his side gasped, staring, as if mesmerized, at the sight of the flames closing in on them.

She wasn't the only one suddenly mesmerized, and for one startling heartbeat, Aidan went utterly still, as for the first time he caught a full glimpse of her.

He knew that profile.

He knew her. *"Kenzie?"*

At the sound of her name on his lips, uttered in a low, hoarse, surprised voice, her head whipped toward his, eyes wide. Her wavy blond hair framed a pale face streaked with dirt and some blood, but was still beautiful, hauntingly so.

She was Mackenzie Stafford, Blake's sister. Kenzie to those who knew and loved her, Sissy Hope to the millions of viewers who watched her on the soap opera *Hope's Passion*.

She was not a stranger to Aidan, but not because of her television stardom. He knew her personally.

*Very* personally. "Kenzie."

"I can't—I can't hear you."

People never expected fire to be noisy, but it was. The flames crackled and roared at near ear-splitting decibels as they devoured everything in their path.

Including them if they didn't move, a knowledge

that was enough to pull his head out of his ass and get with the program. Old lover or not, he still had to get her out of there alive. But she was looking at him through Blake's eyes, and his heart and gut wrenched hard. There was maybe twenty feet of water between *Blake's Girl* and the next boat, which was starting to smoke as well, and would undoubtedly catch on fire any second. It didn't matter. They had no choice. "Kenzie, when I say so, I want you to hold your breath."

"D—do I know you?"

He wore a helmet and all his equipment, and in the dark, not to mention the complete and utter chaos around them, there was no way she could see him clearly. Still, he had to admit it stung. "It's me, Aidan. Hold your breath now, on my count."

"Aidan, my God."

"Ready?"

"The boat's going to go, every inch of it, isn't it?"

Yep, including the few square inches they were standing on. In fact, it was going to go much more quickly than he'd have liked. Since they couldn't get to the dock, it was into the ocean for them, where they'd wait for rescue.

"No," she said, shaking her head. "There's got to be another way."

Unfortunately there wasn't, and he quickly stripped out of his jacket and gear because the protection they offered wouldn't be worth the seventy-five pounds of extra weight while treading water and holding up Kenzie to boot. At least she was conscious. She didn't appear to have on any shoes, or anything particularly heavy on her person, all of which were points in her favor. "On three, okay? Remember to hold your breath."

"I don't think—"

"Perfect. Go with that. One—" He nudged her in front of him, pushing her to the railing.

"Aidan—"

"Two—"

*"Are you crazy?"*

*"Three."*

"Hell, no. I'm not going into the—"

He dropped her into the water, and she screamed all the way down.

# 2

KENZIE HIT THE ICY OCEAN, and as she took in a huge mouthful of water, she realized she'd forgotten to hold her breath, a thought that was completely eradicated when *Blake's Girl* exploded into the early dawn.

In the brilliant kaleidoscope, she barely registered the splash next to her, or the two strong arms that came around her, supporting her as flying pieces of burning debris hit the water all around them.

Aidan. My God, Aidan… That it was him boggled her mind. She tried to remind him that she could swim on her own, but the shock of the cold water sapped both her voice and the air in her lungs, and also hampered the working of her brain.

She'd never experienced anything like it. Never in her life had she been so hot and so frozen at the same time. The heat came from the flames, so high above them now that she was in the water, but no less terrifying. And yet, an icy cold had taken over her limbs, making movement all but impossible, weighing her down, sitting on her chest, sucking the last of the precious air from her overtaxed lungs.

Someone was screaming, and Kenzie envied their ability to draw air into their lungs because her own felt as constricted as if she had a boa slowly squeezing the life out of her.

The scream came again.

*Huh?*

It sounded sort of like her.

And then she realized, as if from a great distance, that it *was* her screaming, which meant that somehow she was breathing. Okay, that was good. So was the man holding her in the water, tucking her head against him, shielding her from the pieces falling out of the sky at his own risk. Without him, she'd have gone down like a heavy stone and she knew it.

"Shh," he was murmuring. "I've got you. It's okay, Kenzie, it's going to be okay…."

She was hurt, but not so hurt as to stop the memories bombarding her at the sound of his voice. How could she not have *instantly* recognized him?

He was the first man who'd ever broken her heart.

He'd ditched his helmet and she could see his face now. He didn't look happy to see her, and honestly, on that point, if he hadn't been saving her sorry ass, they'd have been perfectly in sync. "Aidan." She could see the fire reflected in his eyes. *Blake's Girl* was really blazing now. "My God, we almost—"

"I know." His short, dark hair was plastered to his head. Water ran in rivulets down his face, which was starkly pale. His long, inky-black eyelashes were spiky, and he had a cut above one eyebrow that was oozing blood. In spite of all of that, she had the most ridiculous thought: *wow,* he looked good all fierce and intense and wet.

Aidan Donnelly, first real boyfriend. First…everything…. She could hardly believe it, certainly couldn't process it, so she craned her neck, staring at the boat that looked like one big firecracker. "It just blew, and I—"

"Kenzie—"

"—I mean one minute I'm sitting there missing my brother, and the next…"

He looked into her eyes, his cool and composed. "It's going to be okay, but I need you to—"

"And it blew. I was just sitting there, surrounded by his things, missing him, and then *boom.* My Choos are probably halfway to China by now. I really liked those Choos."

"Kenzie," he said in a tone of authoritative calm. "I need you to listen to me now. Can you do that?"

She could take a gulp of air. But listening? The jury was still out on that one. Her ears were ringing. And the water was so damn cold. In fact, she was shaking and hadn't even realized it, shudders that wracked her entire body and rattled her teeth.

"Hold onto me, Kenzie. That's all you have to do, okay? Just hold onto me."

*Right.* Hold onto him. She'd grown up here in Santa Rey, and once upon a time she'd held onto him plenty. She'd held onto him, laughed with him, slept with him…

Actually, there'd never been much sleeping involved between them, a thought which brought an avalanche of others. Him fresh out of the firefighters' academy and possessing a body that had made her drool, not to mention the knowledge of how to use that body to make hers go wild…

But that had been what, six years ago? Hell, she could barely think, much else handle any math at the moment, so she couldn't be sure.

He was towing her out, away from the boat and any danger of falling debris, while shouting something to two firefighters on the other side of the burning vessel, both of whom had hoses on the fire.

She'd been in a fire before. On the set of her soap opera, *Hope's Passion,* before it'd been cancelled. But that was under carefully controlled circumstances. This wasn't a TV show with lines for her to follow. This was the real thing, with no makeup department standing by to color in pretend injuries, dammit.

She'd have loved a script right about now, with a happy ending, please.

At least she was still breathing.

Hard to beat that.

*Blake's Girl* hadn't gotten so lucky.

Neither had Blake. Oh, yeah, *there* was the familiar rush of pain, slicing right through the numbness from the cold water, lancing her heart—the pain that had been with her since she'd learned Blake was dead. Making it worse, adding confusion and anger to her grief was the fact that he'd been accused of being an arsonist and murderer.

*God, Blake…*

Another chunk of burning debris fell from the still flaming boat, and she imagined it was something of Blake's, something she'd never see again. Or maybe it was her own suitcase, or her laptop, which wasn't a big loss in the scheme of things, but it held the scripts she'd been writing…

At least if she died, she would no longer be a freshly unemployed soap star.

It was so damn ironic—she'd never been able to come home when Blake had been alive because she'd been too busy working. Then days after he'd died, her soap had been cancelled. Now she could drive up all she wanted, and he was gone…. Her first trip home in forever and it had been to see after his things, things that were now smoldering in the water around her.

"Don't give up on me," Aidan said. His eyes focused ahead on where he was swimming to, some point invisible to her. It was too dark to see their color clearly but she knew them to be a light brown with flecks of green that danced when he laughed.

He wasn't laughing now.

*Nope.*

He glanced at her, then resumed swimming straight and sure, moving them away from the flames, which also meant away from any warmth, while she did as he'd asked and just held on. She could do nothing but. Like old times…

Why did it have to be *him,* the guy who'd crushed

her heart, stomped on her pride and then walked away from her without a backward glance?

Did *he* hurt over the loss of Blake?

Did *he* believe the lies?

Because that thought, and all the others that came with it, came close to defrosting her, she shoved them aside. The blessed numbness was working for her. She hadn't come to Santa Rey in the past six years, but Blake had visited her in L.A. on the set, whenever he could, and on top of his visits, they'd been in frequent contact by e-mail, texting and phone calls, and had remained close despite their physical distance. He was the only family she'd had.

And now he was gone.

Forever gone.

"Kenzie? You still with me?" Aidan's lean jaw was tight with tension and was scruffy, as if he hadn't had time to shave in a day or two. Or four.

"Unfortunately." She'd like to be anywhere but "with" him. She could feel his longer, stronger legs moving, bumping into hers, and it made her irrationally mad. She didn't want help, not from him, but when she wriggled free to prove herself fine, she went down like a stone. Straight beneath the surface of the icy water, where she promptly did the stupid thing of opening her mouth to breathe and got a lungful of extremely cold salt water for her efforts.

Thankfully, she was immediately hauled back up again and pulled against a hard chest, one hand fisted in the back of her shirt, the other arm across the backs of her thighs in a grip that could have rivaled Superman's.

Firefighter to victim.

Not ex-boyfriend to ex-girlfriend.

And wasn't that just the problem? Once upon a time he *really* had had her, only he'd been the one to let go. He'd done it, he'd said, because of their respective careers and because he didn't like hiding their relationship from his friend Blake, but she knew the truth. It was because he'd decided she'd been falling in love with him and he hadn't been ready for love, so he'd shooed her away and had moved on.

She'd hated him for that for a good long time, for not giving himself a chance to feel what she'd felt, and, yeah, he'd been right—she *had* been more than halfway in love with him. It'd taken a while, but eventually her anger had drained, and she'd acknowledged that he'd been right to break it off with her before she'd gotten even more hurt…. But that hadn't eased her pain at the time.

Maybe she should consider herself lucky they were doing this reintroduction in an official capacity—him on the job, and her being just one in a blur of people he rescued. Less personal.

"Stop fighting me." His voice cut through the shocking noise of the night: the sirens, the shouting of the other firefighters and personnel, the ever-present, horrifying crackling of the flames, the small waves smacking into each other, waves that would be cresting over her head if it wasn't for Aidan's holding her with what appeared to be little to no effort. "I've got you."

"I don't want you to have me."

"Okay, roger that. But at the moment you don't have a choice."

"Of all the firefighters in this damn town…"

She thought she caught a flash of a grim smile. So he was no more thrilled than she was. He wasn't even looking directly at her, his attention instead focused on the boat behind her, and the dock behind that, reminding her that not only was he saving her hide, he was simultaneously looking for other people who needed help.

"I was alone on the boat," she told him.

"What were you doing?"

"Saying good-bye to Blake."

Sorrow, regret, and anguish all briefly flashed in his eyes. "Kenzie—"

"He didn't do those things you're all accusing him of, Aidan."

She had his attention now, all of it, and she'd forgotten the potency of having Aidan Donnelly giving her one-hundred-percent of his focus. *"He didn't."*

"Did he say something, anything to you at all, before he died?"

Died… Hearing the words from his mouth made Blake's death all the more real, as did being back here in her hometown, and it hit her hard. Throat so tight that she couldn't speak, she shook her head. No, Blake hadn't said anything at all, which made her feel even worse. "It wasn't him who set those fires. I know it."

"Kenzie," he said very gently, but she didn't want to hear it, didn't want to hear anything he said, so she shook her head again and closed her eyes, which brought an unexpected and horrifying sense of vertigo, making her clutch at him. "I want out."

"I know. They're coming for us right now."

That was good. Because something was definitely wrong. Her vision was getting fuzzy. Her brain was getting fuzzier. Scared and a little overwhelmed, she pressed her face into the crook of his neck, her nose to his throat, the position hauntingly familiar and at once flooding her with memories.

She'd been here before.

Okay, not here, not in the water, freezing, scared, but she'd been held by him, had pressed her face against his warm flesh and inhaled him in, absorbing the way he held her close, as if he'd never let anything happen to her.

He smelled the same, a scent she'd never quite managed to forget, and it was messing with her brain in spite of the fact that she'd just survived an explosion, a nighttime swim in the freezing ocean, and an uncomfortable reunion with the one and only guy she'd ever let break her heart.

*Dammit.* She blamed Blake. *Blake...*

"Kenzie." Aidan gave her a little shake. "Stay with me now."

*No, thanks...*

"Open your eyes," he demanded. "Come on, Kenzie. Stay awake, stay with me."

As opposed to giving in to the delicious lethargy slowly taking over? *Nah...* "Too tired."

"I know, but you can do this. You can do anything, remember?"

She nearly smiled at the reminder of her own personal motto, but then remembered who was talking. Yeah, she'd once believed that she could do anything, with him at her side.

He'd proved her wrong.

*Oh, boy.* Her eyes *were* closing. It'd be so easy to let them, to just drift off and not feel the cold anymore, but even in her fuzziness, she knew that was bad, so with great effort, she pried her eyes open.

And her gaze landed on him. The last time she'd seen him, she'd been so young. *They'd* been so young. She'd just turned twenty-two, been signed by a Los Angeles agent, and had landed her first small walk-on role. He'd been two years older, fit and gorgeous, and on top of his world as a young firefighter.

Plastered against him, her hands clenched on his biceps, her legs entwined with his, her chest up against him the way it was, she could feel that he was still fit.

Very fit.

And thanks to the flames and also the spotlights from the guys on the dock keeping track of them, she also knew that he was still gorgeous. If he hadn't cut her loose without a backward glance, she'd be happy to see him.

*Very* happy.

A group of firefighters had made their way through the flames to the end of the neighboring dock, and had secured it with criss-crossing lines of water. One of them leaped into the ocean, and with long, sure strokes swam toward them.

"Here," he called out to Aidan, holding out an arm for Kenzie.

"I've got her," Aidan said.

But Kenzie had had enough, of Aidan and his capable, strong arms, of his scent and especially of the memories. So she reached out for the second fire-fighter, going into his arms without looking back, arms that had never held her before, arms that didn't know her, arms that didn't evoke the past.

Even though she wanted to, she wouldn't look back.

# 3

BY THE TIME AIDAN HAULED himself out of the water, Ty had handed Kenzie off to the EMTs. Dustin and Brooke took her away from the flames and straight to their ambulance.

*Good.*

Chilled, drenched to the skin, Aidan made his way through the organized mayhem to his rig, where he stripped down and pulled on dry gear, the questions coming hard and fast in his head.

What the hell had Kenzie been doing there? Odd timing, given that in all these years, she'd not shown up in Santa Rey, not once. At least that he was aware of. Blake had never mentioned any visits, but then again, why would he? He'd had no idea that Aidan had dated his baby sister, and then walked away rather than engage his heart. They'd never told him, knowing he wouldn't have liked it.

Nope, Kenzie hadn't been back, not even for Blake's memorial service, and yet suddenly here she was, on Blake's boat, a boat that just happened to blow sky high once she'd set foot on it.

Odd coincidence.

During the time the two of them had been in the water together, the sky had lightened. Dawn had arrived. The chief had put an explosives team in place, and had a plan to contain the fire. Aidan needed to get back into the thick of it, but first he had to see Kenzie and make sure for himself that she was okay. She'd had a head laceration and multiple cuts and wounds, and that had been before he'd tossed her into the water.

He looked through the horde of people working the flames—Eddie and Sam, Aaron, Ty and Cristina, plus the guys from Thirty-Three, all on hoses and past the explosives experts surveying the still burning shell of *Blake's Girl* to where the ambulance was parked.

Kenzie was seated at the back of the opened rig between Dustin and Brooke. She was dripping everywhere, her clothes revealing what he already knew, that she was petite and in possession of a set of mouth-watering curves that had gotten only more mouth-watering in the past few years. She wore layered tees, the top one pink, ribbed and long-sleeved, unbuttoned to her waist, the one beneath white with pink polka-dots, opened to just between her breasts, both soaked through and suctioned to her body enough to expose her bra, which was also pink, lace and quite sheer.

He'd been a firefighter for years and he'd rescued countless victims, many female, some of whom had been as wet as Kenzie, and never, not one single goddamn time, had he ever stopped in the middle of a job to notice their breasts.

It was his first clue that he was in trouble, deep trouble—but when it came to Kenzie, that was nothing new. He chose to ignore his observation for now, for as long as he possibly could. His gaze dropped past her shirt with shocking difficulty, to a pair of button-fly jeans low on her hips, also dangerous territory because he'd always loved her legs, especially how bendy they could get….

*Don't go there.*

She shoved her hair out of her face, which still looked far too pale, even a little green, although that didn't take away from her beauty. Once upon a time she'd been a gorgeous study of sexy, frou-frou feminine mystery to him.

Some things never changed.

As if she felt his gaze, she looked up, and from fifty feet, between which were other firefighters, equipment and general chaos, she found him.

Between them the air seemed to snap, crackle, pop.

Six years ago, the thought of a long-distance relationship had been as alien to him as a close-distance relationship, and he'd told himself he had no choice but to break things off, even though that had really just been an excuse.

He'd broken things off because she'd scared him, she'd scared him deep. And apparently, given the hard kick his heart gave his ribs, she still did.

She'd been able to get inside him, make him feel things that hadn't been welcome, and, yeah, he'd run like a little girl.

He felt like running now.

But this time it was Kenzie who turned away. Dustin unfolded a blanket and wrapped it around her shoulders, while Brooke checked her pupils, then dabbed at the various cuts on her face.

Kenzie sat still, eyes closed now, looking starkly pale but alive.

Alive was good.

She huddled beneath the blanket, cradling a wrist, nodding to something Brooke asked her. Aidan knew that Brooke and Dustin, both close friends, would take good care of her. They took good care of everyone, which meant that Kenzie was in the very best hands.

Still in the thick of the organized chaos around him, Aidan took a second to let his gaze sweep over her. She really did seem as okay as he could hope for, and he told himself to turn away.

He was good at that. After all, he'd learned to do so at a young age from his own family, who'd shuffled him around more than a deck of cards on poker night. Yeah, he was good at walking away. Or at least good at pretending he didn't care when others walked away from him.

And after all, he'd done the same to her.

God, he'd been cruel to her all those years ago. Not that he'd meant to be. Going through the academy had been a life lesson for him. He *could* belong to a "family." He *could* make long-lasting friends. He *could* love someone with all his heart.

But loving his fellow firefighters like the brothers they'd become was one thing.

Loving Kenzie had been another entirely.

Since she'd left, he'd seen her only on TV. As a rule, he didn't watch soaps. He didn't watch much TV at all, actually. If he wasn't working, he was renovating the fixer-upper house he'd bought last year, emphasis on *fixer-upper.* If he wasn't doing that, he was playing basketball, or something else that didn't cost any money because the fixer-upper had eaten his savings.

But there'd been the occasional night where he'd sat himself in front of a game and caught a promo for Kenzie's soap. There'd also been the few times at the station where one of the guys had flipped on the TV during her show.

Three times exactly—and yeah, he remembered each and every one. The first had been five years ago, and she'd been wearing the teeniest, tiniest, blackest, stringiest bikini in the history of teeny-tiny black string bikinis, her hair piled haphazardly on top of her head with a few wild curls escaping, looking outrageously sexy as she'd seduced her on-screen lover. It'd taken him a few attempts to get the channel changed, and even then it hadn't mattered. That bikini had stuck with him for a good long while.

The second time had been a few Christmases back. She'd been wearing a siren-red, slinky evening dress designed to drive men absolutely wild. She'd been standing beneath some mistletoe, looking up at some "stud of the month." Aidan hadn't been any quicker with the remote that time, and had watched the entire, agonizing kiss.

The third time had been for the daytime Emmys. She'd accepted her award, thanking Blake for always believing in her, and then had thanked some guy named Chad.

Chad.

What kind of a name was Chad?

And where was Chad now, huh? Certainly not hauling her off a burning boat and saving her cute little ass. Guys named Chad probably only swam when playing water polo.

In the ambulance, Dustin said something to Kenzie, and she opened her eyes, flashing a very brief smile, but it was enough.

She was okay.

Aidan forced himself to move, to get back to the job at hand, and it was a big one. The explosions had caught the boats on either side of *Blake's Girl,* escalating the danger and damages. They had the dock evacuated, and as the sun streaked the sky, they were working past containment, working to get the flames one-hundred-percent out.

With one last look at Kenzie, Aidan entered the fray.

IT TOOK HOURS.

Aidan and his crew piled into their rigs just as the lunch crowd began to clutter the streets of Santa Rey. If he closed his eyes, he could still feel the imprint of Kenzie in his arms. He'd held onto her for what, three minutes tops? And yet she'd filled his head and his senses, and for those one-hundred-and-eighty seconds, time had slipped away, making him feel like that twenty-four-year-old punk he'd once been.

He'd been with Kenzie for one glorious summer, and she'd wanted to stay with him, which should have been flattering. She'd wanted to wear his ring and have a house and a white picket fence.

And his children.

But it hadn't been flattering at all. It'd been terrifying.

So he'd acted like a stupid, shortsighted guy. There was no prettying that up, or changing the memory. Fact was fact. He'd gotten a great job, and he'd had the world at his feet, including, he'd discovered, lots of women who found his chosen profession incredibly sexy.

He'd not been mature enough to realize what he already had; he'd been a first-class asshole. He'd sent Kenzie away, pretended not to look back and had filled his life with firefighting, women, basketball, woodworking, more women…

A hand clasped his shoulder. "Hey, Mr. 2008. Home sweet home."

"Shut up." They'd pulled into the station. He hopped out of the rig and went straight to Dustin, who was cleaning out the ambulance. "The victim? How is she?"

Cristina poked her head out from the station kitchen. "Hey, guys, there's food—" At the sight of Dustin, who she'd gone out with several times before unceremoniously discarding him without explanation, she broke off. "Oh. *You're* here."

Dustin looked at her drily. "What, is the food only for the staff that you *haven't* slept with and dumped?"

Aidan winced at the awkward silence, and if he wasn't in such a desperate hurry to hear about Kenzie, he might have refereed for the two of them, because if anyone needed refereeing, it was these two. "The vic," he said again to Dustin.

"Sorry," Dustin said, turning back to him. "She's not bad, thanks to your quick thinking. A few second-degree burns, possible broken wrist, some lacerations."

"Her head trauma—"

"No concussion."

"Stitches?" he demanded, causing Dustin to take a quick glance at Cristina, who raised an eyebrow.

Aidan knew he was bad off when the two of them could share a worried look over him.

"No stitches," Dustin said. "You okay?"

"Yeah." Aidan took his first deep breath in hours, which prompted another long look between Dustin and Cristina.

"You sure?" Cristina asked.

*Jesus.* "*Yes.*" Leaving them alone to work through their issues, he headed inside the station. After he'd showered, cleaned up and clocked out, he got into his truck and debated with himself.

Home and oblivion were attractive choices.

Or he could go to the hospital, see Kenzie and get a question or two answered.

Not quite as attractive, because nothing about sitting with Kenzie and looking into her soulful eyes was going to be simple. Nope, that was a guaranteed trip to Heartbreak City.

Home, then, where he wouldn't have to do anything but fall facedown into his bed. Yeah, sounded good. He put his truck in gear.

And drove to the hospital.

KENZIE OPENED HER EYES and stared at a white ceiling. She was on a cot in the emergency room, her cuts and burns all cleaned and bandaged, her wrist wrapped, her head stitched back on—okay, so it'd only needed butterfly bandages. Now she was being "observed," although for what, she had no idea.

At least she was warm again, or getting there. She had three blankets piled on top of her, which helped, and a hospital gown, which didn't.

She'd just seen the fire investigator, Mr. Tommy Ramirez. Tommy was short, dark, and quite to the point. The point being that he'd found it extremely odd that she'd been on Blake's boat at the time of its explosion.

She did, too, considering she'd only gotten to town that night. Closing her eyes, she frowned. She also found it odd that he was wasting his time questioning her instead of investigating the real perpetrator of the arsons, because her brother was *innocent*. No way had Blake set all those awful fires they were trying to pin on him. Blake, sweet, quiet, loving Blake, the brother who'd been there for her when their parents had died fifteen years ago, when they'd gone through foster care, when she'd wanted to go off to Hollywood. He'd never have hurt a fly much less purposely hurt another human being. And endanger a child?

Never.

God, she hated hospitals. They smelled like fear and pain and helplessness, and all of them combined reminded her of her own uncertain childhood. She wished she was back on the L.A. set of *Hope's Passion,* acting the part of the victim instead of really being one. Comfort food would help. Maybe a box of donuts—

From the other side of her cubicle curtain came a rustling, and then the hair at the back of her neck suddenly stood up, as if she was being watched. Opening her eyes, she blinked the room into focus. Everything was white and…*blurry.* But not so much so that she missed the back of a guy's head as he ran off and out of sight. "Hey!"

He hadn't been wearing scrubs but a red T-shirt, so he couldn't have been hospital staff. Who'd come to see her and then leave without a word? She struggled to think but she was so tired, and a little woozy still, and when she let her eyes drift shut, she ended up dozing off…

"NOT THE SAME TYPE of point of origin as the other fires."

Kenzie opened her eyes and turned her head, taking in the curtain, now pulled all the way closed around her cot. She was a woman who liked change, who in fact thrived on it, but she had to say, she didn't like this change. Not at all.

How much time had passed?

"So you're saying what, Tommy, that the chief has you on a gag order?"

*Oh, boy.* She didn't need to peek around the curtain to know *that* voice. That voice had once been the stuff of her daydreams, of her greatest fantasies. That voice had used to melt her bones away and rev her engines.

*Aidan.*

"I'm not saying anything," Tommy said. "Except what I told Zach weeks ago. I'm on this. It's a kid glove case. So you need to back off."

"I want to see Kenzie when she wakes up."

*He'd* been the one who'd looked in on her? She didn't know how she felt about that. Had he seen her sleeping? Had she been snoring?

Why hadn't he come back when she called out?

"Tell me this much at least," Aidan said, presumably still to Tommy. "Did either you or the chief even know Blake had a boat?"

"No, but I was waiting on a full investigative report from the county, and it would have shown up on there."

"And then you would've what, seized the property as evidence?"

"Yes, of course. To search it, just like we've done with his house. All the current evidence regarding the case points to Blake being in on the arson."

*In on the arson.* Kenzie absorbed the odd choice of words. Did he mean that he thought there could be more than one arsonist?

"So who beat you to the boat, Tommy? Who wanted to make sure there was no chance of extracting any evidence from it?"

The answer actually gave Kenzie hope—because it

meant that someone *else* could possibly be proven to be responsible for the arsons, maybe even someone who'd framed Blake.

"There's been at least seven highly destructive fires," Tommy said. "Adding up to millions of dollars in damages. The chief's ass is on the line, and so is mine. If Blake was still alive, he'd be behind bars. That he's not doesn't change anything. The investigation is ongoing."

"But it's possible he was working with someone," came Aidan's voice. "Is that what you're saying?"

"No comment."

"Do you know who?"

*"No comment."*

"You know something's off, Tommy, or you wouldn't be here."

"Yes," the investigator agreed tightly. "Something is off, and…"

Their voices lowered to a whisper. She leaned toward the curtain, but they were talking so quietly now she couldn't hear anything but…her name. Definitely, she'd heard her name.

Why were they talking about her?

She scooted even closer to the edge of the cot and cocked an ear, but still couldn't hear anything. *Dammit!* Blake couldn't have done any of those things they'd accused him of. She knew it, and she was going to prove it herself if necessary, starting with eavesdropping on this conversation. Tommy said something Kenzie couldn't quite catch, so she leaned even further, and—

Fell off the cot to the floor. *"Ouch."*

At the commotion, the curtain whipped open. She tried to push herself upright but with one wrist useless and the other pinned beneath her, she was pretty much a beached fish. A nearly naked beached fish, with her butt facing a crowd of three: Tommy, the nurse and, oh, perfect—Aidan. She could see the tabloids now: Ex-Soap Star Mackenzie Caught Panty-less. "Ouch," she said again and rolled to her back, gasping when the cold linoleum hit her bare backside. She sighed just as someone dropped to his knees at her side, and then Aidan's face swam into her vision.

"Are you okay?" he demanded.

*Sure.* Sure, she was okay. If she didn't think about the fact that she'd just mooned him.

"Here." After helping him get her back on the cot, the nurse fussed a moment, checking all of Kenzie's various injuries. Luckily, Tommy had backed out of the room, vanishing, for now at least.

"What the hell were you doing?" Aidan demanded when the nurse left them alone, too.

"Oh, a little of this, a little of that—" Realizing her gown was twisted very high up on her thighs—which, of course, was nothing to what he'd just seen—she grabbed her blanket and tried to cover herself up. A little like closing the barn door after the horse had escaped, she knew, but she was mortified. Except the movement made her want to throw up, and she reached up, holding her head tightly.

"Here." He took over the task of covering her,

quickly extricating his hands when he was done, not quite meeting her gaze as he sat at her side.

Awkward moment… "So," she said. "What are you doing here?"

"Looking in on you."

Yep. And he'd gotten to look in on far more than he'd probably intended.

"Are you all right?" he asked.

"Depends on your definition of *all right.*"

At that, his eyes cut to hers and he sighed, scrubbing a hand over his face, his fingers rasping over the growth there. He looked and sounded exhausted. "I'm sorry, Kenzie."

"For what? That I just mooned you, or that I'm here at all?"

Aidan got to his feet, pulling the curtain shut again to give them privacy, privacy that she wasn't sure she wanted.

He'd changed his clothes. He wore a pair of jeans now, loose on his long legs, low on his hips, with a long-sleeved shirt unbuttoned over a gray T-shirt that seemed to emphasize his broad shoulders and tough, athletic build. "Your shirt isn't red," she said slowly.

"What?"

"Before, somebody in a red shirt was looking at me."

"When?"

"I don't know." She rubbed her temples. "I'm out of it."

"It was a tough night."

"Yeah." But *he* didn't look like he'd just worked his

ass off and managed to save her life to boot; he looked casual, relaxed.

Cool as a cucumber.

And so hauntingly familiar, not to mention gorgeous, that she couldn't keep her eyes on him. How unfair was it that he'd gotten even better-looking with age? "Thanks for stopping by, Aidan, but you can see I'm fine. You can go."

He looked doubtful.

"Seriously. I'm really okay."

She almost had him, she could tell, but then she ruined it by shivering.

Without a word, he grabbed another blanket and settled it over her. She appreciated his sense of duty, but what she would appreciate even more would be his vanishing.

Or her.

Yeah, that might be better. If she could just vanish on the spot. *Poof.* "Okay, now I'm good, thanks. Really."

"Really?"

"Yes. I mean you can't even look at me, so—"

Lifting his head, he met her eyes, his hot enough to singe her skin.

"Oh," she breathed, feeling her heart kick, hard.

"I can't look at you?" he repeated in low disbelief. "Are you kidding me? Kenzie, I can't do anything *but* look at you."

# 4

AT AIDAN'S WORDS, Kenzie's breath caught and held. She didn't know how to take him, especially the way he was looking at her, as if maybe he could see all the way through her, to her heart and soul, right to the very center of her being, where all the hurt was so carefully bottled up.

She'd gotten over him. Years ago. She really had. She'd gotten over how he'd once made her laugh, made her think, made her happy…

Made her come…

No way could he possibly reach her now. Not with that hard body, not with the look in his eyes and definitely not with the memories.

Okay, maybe the memories got to her, just a little bit. For one glorious summer, he'd been the best part of her life—before he'd walked away without so much as a glance back, that is.

*Good. There* was her anger, which would hopefully negate the fact that he was standing right here in the flesh looking good enough to…well… That thought made her want to sweat. But apparently she could be both over him and turned on by him at the same time, which confused her to say the least. She had no idea what that was about. No idea at all.

*None.*

She'd moved on years ago from that young, sweet, innocent girl. Now she was a woman with a backbone of sheer steel that had gotten her through some tough times.

She knew people tended to look at her carefully cultivated outer package—thank you, stylist to the stars—an outer package that was petite and willowy, even fragile-looking, and completely underestimate her.

But on the inside she was one-hundred-percent survivor, thank you very much. She'd lived through losing her parents early, through a happy-as-it-could-be teenage-hood with just Blake. She'd lived through being in the public eye, through the ups and downs of TV fame and most recently, through the death of her brother. All of that would have cracked most women, but she wasn't easily cracked.

She would get to the bottom of this mess, no matter what she had to do in order to get there. *No matter what.* Even if she had to use her beauty, her checking account, her damn body.

She would do it.

Whatever it took.

*For Blake.*

"I heard you talking to the investigator," she said softly.

Aidan's eyes met hers, and she wished like hell she

could read his mind. But she couldn't, and he didn't say another word to help.

"I think he's wondering if I'm guilty of something."

He just looked at her some more.

"The only thing I'm guilty of is knowing that he hasn't done his job if he thinks Blake did those things."

At that, his face softened, and regret filled his eyes, along with a grimness that had her shaking her head before he even spoke.

"Don't say it," she warned, not willing to hear it, not from him. Not from anyone. Not when she was this close to a breakdown. A grief breakdown. "Don't." She *knew* Blake, goddammit. She did. She didn't remember much about her parents before they'd died in a car crash, but she remembered Blake. Every bit of him. He was the boy who'd held her hand every time they'd had to move to a new foster home. He was the teenager who'd punched a boy in the face when he'd hurt her, he was the man who'd believed in her enough to work double shifts to pay for her publicity shots so she could pursue her acting dream.

He could *never* have committed arson. She'd have sworn Aidan would have known that as well, but apparently she was wrong.

"There's evidence—" he began, but she shook her head.

"Circumstantial." She swallowed hard but a lump of emotion, the one that had been there since Blake's death, remained. "I see that you're no better a friend than you were a boyfriend."

He opened his mouth, but before he could respond, the nurse pulled aside the curtain and entered the cubicle, followed by a doctor. "Everyone out," the nurse ordered.

"I'm the only one here," Aidan said.

"So get out," the nurse responded sweetly.

Kenzie closed her eyes and lay back. She didn't look at Aidan again; in fact, she didn't open her eyes until she heard the rustling of the curtain, signaling he'd left.

Which was fine. Perfect, really. Because she'd sure as hell rather be alone than look into his eyes and see things she didn't want to see.

AIDAN EXITED the emergency room, feeling like a class-A jerk. Though how that was possible, what with his saving her life and all, he had no idea....

Okay, he knew.

She'd seen the look in his eyes; she'd understood something she hadn't wanted to understand—that he knew Blake was involved with those arson fires.

Aidan felt torn up about it, sick over it, but facts were facts. Blake had been placed at the scene of each arson by various witnesses. He had been depressed since losing Lynn, his partner before Cristina, in a fire the year before. His home had been seized and searched, and in his garage they'd found a stack of wire mesh trash cans, similar to the ones identified as the point of origin in each of the arsons.

Most damning, Aidan's partner, Zach, had also seen

him holding a blowtorch just moments after Zach's house had been set on fire, with Zach and Brooke inside. Zach had almost died there.

And Blake *had* died there, perhaps deliberately. He'd died, leaving all of them, Zach, Aidan and the other firefighters, even Tracy, the woman he'd had such a crush on, everyone, destroyed.

Kenzie was in denial. He got that. She was angry. He got that, too. She needed someone to vent that anger at, to place it on, and he'd been handy enough.

*I see that you're no better a friend than you were a boyfriend.*

Yeah, that had been a direct hit. Having her look at him as if *he* was the bad guy had really gotten to him, especially considering he still had the scrapes and bruises from saving her.

The late afternoon sun was sinking fast, cooling off the day. Having been up for two straight days now, he desperately needed sleep. He could close his eyes standing up right there in the hospital lot, and not wake up if a cyclone hit. He was so tired that he'd probably sleep completely dreamless. Well, except for maybe dreaming about Kenzie's bare ass. Yeah, now that he'd seen that again, he'd most likely dream about it for a good many hours.

Days.

Years.

"Aidan."

*Hell.* Tommy was leaning up against Aidan's truck, a file in his hands, mouth pinched tight, looking as if he had plenty of things to say, and all fantasies about Kenzie's ass vanished. "What now?"

"I wasn't aware that you knew her personally."

"Who?"

"Come on, Aidan. Don't play with me. Mackenzie Stafford. You didn't say that you knew her."

He sighed. "So?"

"So it felt to me like maybe you knew her…*well*."

"Yeah. Once upon a time."

"Okay, and so once upon a time, did you know she was Blake's sister?"

Getting into tricky territory here. No one had known he and Kenzie had dated in the past. It'd been a quick, hot thing, *very* hot, and he certainly hadn't been in any hurry to tell Blake he'd gotten his sister in bed. Kenzie hadn't told Blake, either, for her own reasons, and then when Kenzie had gone off to Los Angeles, it hadn't mattered anymore.

Did it matter now, with Blake dead? He couldn't see how it did. "Yeah, I knew she was Blake's sister."

"Did you know that boat was Blake's?"

"Where are we going with this, Tommy?"

"Did you?"

Aidan let out a breath. "Not until we were in the water and she told me."

Tommy nodded. "Because you always sit around with someone you're rescuing and chat about property ownership."

"I asked her why she was there, on that boat. I was under the impression that she was in Los Angeles."

"Yeah?" Tommy's eyes studied him, considering. "So just how well do you know her?"

"Irrelevant."

"I wonder if Blake would have thought so."

Aidan fished his keys out of his pocket. "I'm going home to sleep. For many, many hours. When I'm back on duty you can drill me all you want. Maybe I'll be able to think more clearly."

"Maybe I don't want you thinking more clearly."

"And what the hell does that mean?"

"It means I need answers now. Did you know she was staying on the boat? Did you maybe visit with her there before the fire?"

"I told you. No. And no."

"Ms. Stafford thinks Blake is innocent. That he was not only framed but possibly murdered, and she intends to prove it."

*Sounded right.* Kenzie might look like a pretty ball of fluff, but she had sharp wits and was loyal to a fault. She also had the tenacity of a bulldog. Once she got her brain wrapped around an idea, there was nothing anyone could do to change her mind. Not about falling in love with him, not about being an actress and most definitely not about believing that Blake couldn't be guilty of arson.

"So the question stands," Tommy said quietly. "How well do you know her?"

"Did." Well enough that when he'd looked into her eyes, he'd felt an odd stirring, a sensation almost like coming home. Yeah, once upon a time he'd known her well. As well as he'd known anyone. "Past tense."

"Good enough."

"For what?"

"To get you to tell her to stay the hell out of this investigation and not interfere."

"People don't tell Kenzie what to do."

"You're going to. Because the chief has put out the word. If anyone hinders this investigation, we'll have them arrested, Blake's sister or not."

*Great. Perfect.* If Aidan told her that, she'd jump in with both feet, because one thing he remembered and remembered well—nothing scared her. Nothing. "Seriously. It's not a good idea for me to tell her anything."

"Well, then, I hope she has bail money."

*Shit.* Aidan watched Tommy walk away, then he turned to his truck. Needing sustenance before he passed out cold for at least the next twelve hours straight, he stopped at Sunrise, the café that was the perpetual hangout for everyone at the station. The two-story building was right on the beach. Downstairs was food central, while the second floor was the living quarters for Sheila, the owner. The rooftop was the place to go to view the mountains, the ocean, the entire world it seemed, and to think.

Stepping inside, his sense of smell immediately filled with all the aromas he associated with comfort: coffee, burgers, pies… Sheila smiled at him, and as the sixty-two-year-old always did, fawned over him as he imagined a mother would.

His own mother wasn't too into fawning, at least not over him. She'd divorced his father when Aidan had been two, and he'd spent most of his childhood years being shuffled from family member to family member while she'd relived her wild youth. Granted, he'd been more than a handful of trouble, purposely going after it in a pathetic bid for attention, so in hindsight he didn't blame anyone for not keeping him around for long.

Eventually, he'd ended back up at his dad's, where the two of them had spent a few years doing their best to tolerate each other until, when Aidan had been fifteen, his dad had remarried and promptly given his new wife three babies in a row.

Aidan had landed at his mom's once again, a little bit rebellious and a lot angry, but by then his mother had settled down some, remarrying as well.

Now Aidan had five half brothers and sisters, and didn't quite belong on either side of the family.

Not that he'd had it as rough as Blake and Kenzie had. He knew exactly why the brother and sister had been as close as they had, and exactly why Kenzie would fight tooth and nail to prove her brother's innocence.

What he didn't know was how to convince her to let the law handle things, or if he even had a right to ask such a thing of her.

Between a rock and a hard place.

He ate his fill, and by the time he set down his fork, he felt halfway human. He still needed his bed, badly, but with Tommy's words echoing in his head, he knew he had to try to talk to Kenzie again first. He needed to warn her to let Tommy do his job. For old times' sake.

Or so he told himself.

He pulled out his cell phone and called the hospital, but was told she'd been released.

Where would she go? Back to Los Angeles? No, she wouldn't leave Santa Rey, not until she did what she'd come to do, which was prove Blake's innocence, so he asked Sheila for the local phone book and a slice of key lime pie, both of which he took up to the roof. Sitting facing the ocean, he began calling. But as it turned out, Kenzie wasn't registered at any of the three hotels in the area, probably because there were two conventions in town and everything was fully booked. He looked at the remaining list of several dozen motels and B and Bs, and sighed. He'd made his way through the most likely candidates when Sheila came out on the roof with a fresh mug of coffee.

"What's up for you tonight?" Even with her bouffant hair, she barely came up to his shoulder. "You planning on saving any more damsels in distress?"

He didn't bother asking her how she knew about last night's fire—the gossip train in Santa Rey was infamous. "No damsels, distressed or otherwise. I have a bed in my immediate future."

"You sleeping alone these days?"

*Unfortunately, yeah.* The last woman he'd gone out with had found someone else, someone with more money and more time, and he'd gotten over her fairly quickly but hadn't yet moved on. He couldn't tell that to Sheila, though, or she'd set him up with her niece, as she'd been trying to do all year….

"My niece would be perfect for you, Mr. 2008."

He winced. "You saw the calendar."

"Honey, I saw, I bought, we all drooled. Now about my niece…"

Her niece was divorced with four kids, and while she was a very lovely woman, a waitress at Sunrise, in fact, he wasn't anxious to help create yet another fractured family. "I'm sorry, Sheila. But at the moment, I'm—"

"Enjoying being alone," Sheila finished for him with a sigh. "Yeah, yeah, I've heard it before."

Standing, he handed her back the phone book, then gave her a hug. "How about you? You could marry me."

She cackled good and long over that one, and walked to the roof door. "If I was thirty years younger, you'd be sorry you said that…."

He laughed, but his smile faded fast enough. With no idea how to track down Kenzie, he left and drove home, thinking he'd just go horizontal for a little while and then figure it out, but as he drove up to his house, he saw a red convertible Mercedes Cabriolet in his driveway.

And the outline of a woman sitting on his porch, lit from behind by the setting sun.

She was wearing two hospital gowns layered over each other and a pair of hospital booties, reminding him that her clothes had gotten sliced and diced pretty good and probably any luggage she'd had on the boat was long gone.

Her hair, wild on the best of days, had completely rioted around her face in an explosion of soft waves, the long side bangs poking her in one eye and resting against her cheek and jaw, where she had a darkening bruise that matched the one above her other eye, accompanied by a two-inch-long butterfly-bandaged cut. She was cradling her splinted left wrist in her lap. Her good hand was cut up as well, and so were both her arms—nothing that appeared too deep or serious, but enough to make him wince for her. Her legs were more of the same.

She was alone and beat up, and hell if that didn't grab him by the throat and squeeze. Then there were those melt-me eyes that lifted to his and filled.

*Jesus.* He thought he was so damn tough but one soft sigh from those naked lips and he was a bowl of freaking jelly.

She had a plastic bag beside her, and one peek at it tugged at him harder than he could have imagined given what he did for a living and how often he'd seen this very thing.

Her clothes from the fire.

Probably all that she had left here in Santa Rey. In her unsplinted hand she clutched a small prescription bottle, most likely pain meds. *Hell.* He was such a goner.

"I haven't taken any yet," she whispered, shaking the bottle. "Couldn't, because I took a cab from the hospital to the docks where I had my car, which I drove here."

"Kenzie—"

"You had a package. It was torn, so I looked in." She

lifted one of a stack of firefighter calendars, with his own mug and half-naked body on the cover.

"Nice," she said, a ghost of a smile crossing her lips. "Mr. 2008."

He bit back a sigh. "It's for charity."

"And you definitely contributed." She waggled her eyebrows, then winced. "*Ouch.* I'm not allowed in Blake's house—evidence. And the hotels are all booked up, just my luck. Did you know you have a convention of dog trainers in town? Why are there five hundred dog trainers in Santa Rey?"

"Because we let dogs on our beaches."

"Oh." She sighed. "So we let dogs on our beaches, but not me into a hotel. Kinda makes sense when you think about it."

How that made sense, he had no idea.

"Because my karma sucks."

"Okay, come on." Gently, he pulled her up, taking the bag. Letting her hold onto the medication, he led her inside, telling himself he was going to give her Tommy's warning and that was it.

Other than that, he was going to stay out of it entirely.

But holding onto her, he realized she was trembling, and as he took her into his living room, she went directly for his couch, which she sank onto with a grateful little sigh. "I think she went on vacation."

"Who?"

"My karma." She gave him an exasperated look, like he wasn't listening to her, and then very carefully leaned her head back and closed her eyes.

"Hey." Squatting down before her, he put his hands on her thighs, looking into her eyes when she opened them. "You okay?"

She let out a sound that might have been a laugh, or a sob.

He hoped to God it was the first. "Rough twenty-four hours," he murmured.

Another nod, carefully slow and precise, giving her away. She definitely wasn't laughing. In fact, she was in pain, lots of it; rising, he went into the kitchen for a glass of water. Bringing it back to her, he pried the prescription drugs from her fingers, read the label—yep, painkillers—and shook one out.

"I'm okay."

"You don't look it. You look like hell."

"You say the nicest things."

With another sigh, he once again hunkered down at her side. "Look, you've been through a lot. I know you're alone and…"

"If you say helpless, I'll slug you with my good fist."

Once upon a time she'd been the most amazing thing in his life.

*The. Most. Amazing. Thing.*

On the outside she'd been so mind-blowingly, adorably, effortlessly sexy. Inside, she'd been pure warmth and sweetness, loyal to a fault, always believing the best in everyone, willing to defend what she believed in to the death if necessary.

From their very first moment together, she'd wreaked havoc with his common sense. Before her, nothing in his world had been warm or sweet or particularly loyal. She'd brought lightness into the dark.

Until he'd sent her away. "Not helpless," he said a little thickly. "Never helpless."

"Okay, then." She hugged herself and shivered.

With a frown, he moved to the fireplace. For late summer, the evening did have a chill to it, and she probably was still in some shock. He set up kindling and held a lit match to it until it flamed with a low *whoosh*.

With a startled cry, Kenzie shrank back from the small flames, covering her face.

*Yeah, still in shock.* He should have thought about how she'd feel about a flame of any kind, and cursing himself, he rose and went to her.

"I'm okay," she whispered, peeking out from between her fingers, very carefully not looking at the flickering fire. "It's the crackling." She grimaced. "And, okay, the sight. I don't know what's wrong with me."

"It's normal."

"I don't feel normal."

He didn't feed the small fire, letting it burn out. "I'm sorry. Let's go with the heater instead, okay?"

Once again she leaned her head back, carefully not moving a single inch more than she absolutely had to. "Thanks."

She was killing him. "Kenzie—"

"Could we not talk? It's threatening my head's precarious perch on my shoulders."

"Take the pill."

"I guess I could use a little oblivion. Okay, I could use a lot of oblivion…." Turning her head, she eyed the fireplace as if it were a spitting cobra. "You know, they don't call me Kenzie in Los Angeles."

"Or in the gossip rags."

Without moving another muscle, she arched an eyebrow, appearing to be genuinely surprised. He'd given himself away.

"You read them?"

"Hard to miss when you're going through the grocery store," he said defensively. "They're right next to the candy bars."

The smallest smile crossed her lips.

"You dated that underwear model. The one who danced naked on all the commercials. Chad."

"Chase. And he wasn't naked. He was wearing the underwear he was marketing. Which isn't that much less than what you're wearing in that calendar, Mr. 2008." She gave him a long look.

"Last year you went out with a European prince."

"Now that was just publicity."

He didn't know if he believed her, or cared.

Strike that. He cared. "Take the pill." He watched her chase it with the glass of water he offered.

Yeah, he cared.

*Dammit.*

"Problem," she said, and licked a drop of water off her bottom lip.

He dragged his gaze up to hers. "What?"

"Even if there were no dogs. I still couldn't get a

room. I have no money—my purse either burned up or is below several yards of water, probably both." Kenzie winced. "The hospital had to give me an emergency taxi voucher to get to my car. I'd be really screwed right now if my keys hadn't been in my pocket. Luckily, I also left my cell in the car, so I called my financial manager and he's overnighting emergency funds. But your address was the only one I could think to give him, and I have no place to go until it arrives. And now I can't drive." She shook the bottle of pills. "It's not recommended."

Their eyes met as the implications of her little speech sank in.

"Apparently, I still trust you," she whispered. "At least a little."

*Damn* if that didn't cut right through everything to the heart of the matter. For better or worse, she trusted him, and he had to admit, that meant something to him. Plus, there was the other truth—there was no other place she could go. Like it or not, he was her only contact in town. Which meant…

She was staying here.

With him.

# 5

KENZIE SAT ON AIDAN'S COUCH absorbing the awkward silence. Her eyes were closed but she could feel him close. Thinking. Probably panicking. "Or if you loan me a few bucks, I'll call a cab."

"And go where?"

*Right.* Well, dammit, if he'd just give her some room, she could just sit and try to ignore him—*try* being the key word.

It wasn't his good looks that held her interest. She'd had her fill of good-looking guys on a daily basis at work and she would have said Aidan wasn't that pretty, at least not soap-star pretty. Until she'd seen the calendar. Because holy cow, he'd looked pretty damn fine in eight-and-a-half-by-eleven color glossy, there was no doubt. But he was also tough, and far more rugged than that. There was just something about his eyes and mouth, and the laugh lines lining both that suggested he could be dangerous or outrageous, sweet or maybe not so much, sheer trouble or the boy next door....

She knew all to be true.

What she didn't know was why she'd come *here,* to his house.

Okay, she knew. He was the only familiar thing in her entire world. She'd gotten his address easily enough by calling his station, where some friendly firefighter had recognized her and cheerfully offered up direction. She'd driven here on auto-pilot, having no trouble remembering her way around Santa Rey, getting spooked only when she'd thought she was being followed by a gray sedan.

Which was ridiculous and paranoid. God, she needed a nap.

Aidan's house was tiny, and definitely old, but cozy. From the looks of things, he'd been remodeling it. The living room had lovely hardwood floors and gorgeous wood trim on all the windows, which looked out to the ocean and the rolling hills surrounding it.

He'd always been handy—with tools, with his mind, his words.

His body…

Yeah, he'd been really good in that department. In fact, it was fair to say he'd been her willing tutor, and she a most apt pupil.

But that thought led to others, including the fact that she'd once been young and stupid enough to believe in fairy tales. Aidan had been her prince, her happily-ever-after.

Until he hadn't been.

Luckily she was no longer young or stupid. She no longer dated men while dreaming of that white picket fence and two point four kids. Nope, she dated simply to have fun, and once in a while, to have good sex.

Easy come, easy go.

Too bad she and Aidan weren't having a go at things now, because she was finally with the program, she finally got the rules. They'd probably have a hell of a time.

An evening breeze came through an open window and she drew in a fresh breath. Her pain pill had begun to kick in, and she sank a little deeper into the very comfortable couch. The last time she'd been in Aidan's place, which back then had been an apartment, he'd owned a bed, a TV, a stereo and a box of condoms.

That'd been all they'd needed.

She hadn't been the only one to change. His needs had apparently upgraded. His couch was extra large, and double extra comfortable. There was a TV, triple extra large, and the perennial stereo. But he also had a desk with a computer on it, and some beautiful prints on the walls, which were painted in muted beachy colors.

No condoms in sight. That was undoubtedly for the best. But she liked the house. Low maintenance, calm, even warm and clean. Her place wasn't so different, which meant she felt far more at home here than she would have ever admitted out loud.

How ironic that she'd come back into town to handle Blake's affairs, and to raise hell on the arson charges, intending to stay as far out of Aidan's path as possible, only to end up here in his house, with nowhere else to go.

High on meds...

From the windows she could hear the waves slapping against the shore. Next to her, he was still, just sitting there breathing, soft and even, but she didn't look at him. Wasn't ready to look at him. Yet apparently her nose didn't get that memo because her nostrils quivered, trying to catch a quick whiff of the man—except all she could smell was herself and the smoke and soot stuck to her skin. "I stink."

"It's stress."

"No, not like that." She rolled her eyes, which hurt like a son-of-a-bitch. "Like smoke."

"You could take a shower." His voice was low, a little gritty, and a whole lot suggestive, although she knew that last was all her own imagination.

She couldn't help it, the guy had a voice that brought to mind slow, hot sex. Seriously, if he could bottle the sound, he'd have been rich.

"Kenzie? Do you want to take a shower?"

*Yes, please.* In her own place with her own things and her own thick, cozy, warm bathroom and fuzzy bunny slippers. And then she'd like a good DVD and a bag of popcorn, something to give her mind a mini-vacation from its current hell. "That would be nice, thanks."

He offered her a hand. She stared at it, and then into his face, which was solemnly watching her. "Just a hand," he murmured.

Knowing she was a bit wobbly, she put her hand in his bigger, warmer one and let him pull her up. She staggered into him, and for a moment he held her, and caving in to her own yearning, she pressed her face to his throat and was immediately overcome with memories.

But she didn't do memories, at least not anymore, so she forced herself to step free of him.

He led her down the hall and into what must have been his bedroom. The walls were a soft cream, which went beautifully with the cedar ceilings. But what caught her eye was the biggest bed she'd ever seen, piled high with a thick navy-blue comforter and a mountain of pillows. It was made, sort of. It was *boy*-made, which meant the covers had been tugged up. His hamper appeared to be a pile of clothes in the corner, but other than that, the room was as warm and clean and welcoming as the rest of the house.

She shouldn't have been surprised. The Aidan she'd known had been rough-and-tumble tough, always cool and calm and impenetrable no matter the circumstances, which she imagined served him well in his field. She'd seen that in action on the boat and in the water.

But much like his house, he had a warm, soft, welcoming center. It was what had made him so damn likeable.

Now, with the dubious honor of a few years and some maturing, that likeability had turned into an undeniable sex appeal she discovered while standing there staring at his bed, feeling a rather inexplicable stirring deep in her belly.

"Here." With a hand to the small of her back, he gently nudged her all the way into the room, then passed by her, his arm brushing hers as he moved into the bathroom, which was all cool, white tile and more wood trim. He flipped on the shower, which was nearly as big as his entire kitchen.

"Wow," she said, staring at it.

He shrugged. "I like showers."

"I remember." The words slipped out of her mouth before she could stop them. *Damn,* she really needed a script writer for this real-life thing.

His gaze slid to hers. Very slowly, he arched an eyebrow.

She turned away to blush in peace, but he turned her back toward him with a careful hand on her arm. "Kenzie?"

She stared at his chest, her vision a little compromised by the nice little pill she'd taken, but not so much so that she couldn't appreciate the view. "Yeah?"

"Do we need to talk?"

*Absolutely not.* "No."

She didn't want to discuss her carnal knowledge of his love of showering. Not when she remembered, in vivid Technicolor, taking more than a few with him. She remembered, for instance, the time he'd backed her up to the shower wall in his apartment, lifting her legs around his waist, thrusting into her until she couldn't have told him her own name. She remembered the feel of him, hot and thick inside her, remembered how it felt to be pressed between the hard wall and his harder body, the water pounding down over the top of them until she'd cried out so loudly his roommate had pounded on the bathroom door to make sure she was okay…. They'd laughed so hard they'd barely been able to finish, but they'd managed.

They'd always managed.

The humbling truth was, once upon a time, he'd been able to make her come in less than three minutes, using nothing more than his mouth and his portable showerhead.

*God.*

Just the reminder had her beginning to sweat and her knees wobbling. And if she was being honest, there were some other even more base reactions going on. She firmly ignored them all and lifted her chin. "No. We don't need to talk."

He nodded very solemnly, but she would have sworn his eyes had heated, and along with that heat was a sort of wry humor.

Oh, perfect. Now *he* was remembering, too.

But what really cooked her goose was while she was squirming, nipples hard, thighs trembling, he was amused.

She ought to slug him. She thought about it, but just then, from the plastic hospital bag came the muffled sound of her cell ringing. Since it could only be someone she didn't want to talk to, like her agent wanting her to get in line for auditions before everyone else from her show snatched up all the jobs, she ignored it.

He gestured toward the steaming shower. "It was the first thing I redid in the house."

Thinking about his shower was infinitely more appealing than thinking about being unemployed. Thinking about him *in* the shower? Priceless. But he was still looking just amused enough at her interest that she shrugged lightly. *Look at me not caring...*

But on the inside she was caring big-time, wondering how the hell to get him *un*-amused and hot, because dammit she wanted him hot.

Why the hell she wanted it made no sense to her, none whatsoever, but she couldn't stop thinking about it. *She* was hot, so *he* needed to be the same. Call it petty revenge on the guy who'd once walked away from her. Call it desperation for a diversion from her real reason for being here. But she wanted him to want her. *Needed* him to want her. She wanted that more than her next breath, and she wanted him to suffer for it.

Around them the steam started to rise, but instead of declaring his undying lust for her, he turned and walked back into his bedroom, vanishing from view.

Kenzie let out a breath. Weary, tired of her own smoky stench, she removed her splint and reached for the tie on her hospital gowns, then went still in surprise when Aidan reappeared.

His broad shoulders filling the doorway, his dark eyes met hers as he held out two folded towels. "You still like to use two?"

She blinked as he set them on the counter by the sink. "Yeah." She cleared her throat. "Thanks."

Jaw a little tight, he nodded, and very carefully didn't come any closer.

*Huh.* He didn't look that amused now. He looked, dared she think it, a little…hot.

Interesting.

He was going to give her some privacy. Privacy that, shock of all shocks, she didn't actually want. But there he went, turning away again.

"I'll be in the other room if you need anything," he said. "Just call for me."

*Wow.* He was being considerate, sweet and sensitive, none of the traits she would have associated with him. "You know, this would probably be a lot easier on me if you could continue to be the asshole that you once were."

"Yeah, there's a problem with that."

"Which is?"

"I'm not the same guy I was then."

She opened her mouth, not sure what she planned on saying, but it didn't matter because he walked away, shutting the door quietly behind him.

Kenzie stared at the closed door before stripping and then getting into the shower. Once there, she hissed when the water hit her various cuts but she stood beneath the spray anyway, for a very long time, before finally soaping up. It took five shampoos to get out the smoke smell and even then she wasn't sure she managed completely. By the time the hot water was gone, her skin was wrinkled like a prune and she smelled like Aidan. It was ridiculous but she kept lifting her arm to her nose so she could inhale the scent of him.

When she'd wrapped herself up in the towels, one

on her head, one around her body, she opened the bathroom door and found Aidan sitting on the bed, his legs spread, his hands clasped between them, his face pensive. "Better?" he asked, looking for himself.

"Almost human."

A brief smile curved his lips as he held out bandages and antiseptic cream for her injuries. "I was wondering if you planned on drowning yourself in there."

"I'm angry and frustrated and devastated, but not stupid."

He let out a slow nod, his gaze dropping from her face to her body, studying the towel covering her from just beneath her armpits to mid-thigh. She was gratified to see an absolute lack of humor now.

Slowly he stood up, and something surged within her. Lust, which she beat back. Triumph, which she let take over. *Want me...* Yeah, that worked for her, him wanting her. Because when he admitted that out loud, she was going to lift her chin, flat-out reject him and maybe feel just the tiniest bit better.

She hoped. God, she hoped. Because *something* had to ease this knot in her chest. *Knot, hell.* It was a ball, a huge ball, and it was suffocating her. If she gave too much thought to it, it swelled even bigger and threatened to overcome her.

Then he walked toward her, and she shivered in anticipation because here it came, the him wanting her portion of the evening.

But he simply held out her cell phone. "It went off again when you were in the shower. Local cell number."

"Oh." She flipped it open and looked at it, having no idea who would be calling her locally. Blake had been her last tie to Santa Rey. In any case, whoever it was hadn't left a message so she set the phone down.

Aidan strode right past her, going to his dresser.

Okay, she could work with this. Maybe he was going for a condom. Which of course he wasn't going to need—

He held up a shirt. "You still like to sleep in just a T-shirt?"

She stared at the shirt in his hand, at the hand that had once been able to make her purr. She lifted her head, met his gaze, and smiled.

He gave her a little smile in return, and it was all the more sexy because it was a little baffled, a little bowled over, as if he was surprised, pleasantly so, to find her finally smiling at him.

But she wanted more than that. Needed more than that, and she thought maybe she knew what to do.

If she dared…

But she'd always been bold, especially in front of a camera. And if she closed her eyes, she could be bold here as well.

Doing just that, she then reached up, pulling out the end of the towel from between her breasts, and let the thing drop.

It hit the floor with a soft thud.

Naked as a jay bird, she opened her eyes.

Aidan, unflappable, cool, calm as the eye-of-a-storm Aidan, had gone still as stone, his only movement his Adam's apple when he swallowed hard.

She held out a hand for the proffered T-shirt.

He didn't let go of it, seemingly frozen into place, as he looked her over from head to toes and back again.

She'd never thought of herself as particularly vengeful, and especially didn't wish him harm after he'd saved her life, but he'd once been able to walk away from her without a backward glance, and that had not only broken her heart, but destroyed her confidence.

The look on his face took a good part of that remembered pain away. "Thank you," she said, tugging on the T-shirt, practically having to pry it out of his fingers.

He didn't say a word, he didn't have to. The bulge behind the button fly of his jeans said it all, and with a little shimmying movement, she pulled the shirt over her head, letting it cover her body, before turning and walking out of the room, a real smile on her face for the first time since she'd heard about Blake's death.

# 6

THE MOMENT HE WAS ALONE in his bedroom, Aidan let
out a long, slow breath. He needed to go after Kenzie
to tell her she could have his bed to sleep in, but after
the past sixty seconds, he needed a moment.

Or ten.

Or maybe a cold shower.

Bending for the towel she'd dropped, he winced.
Still hard as a rock, but who wouldn't be? She had the
body that most red-blooded males fantasized about—
all soft, warm curves, and then there'd been her tan
lines, outlining what looked like a string bikini.

God bless tan lines.

Yeah, he was going to need another moment. He
calculated a few multiplication problems in his head,
and then went after her. She stood in his living room
with her back to him, facing the large picture window
that looked out on a darkening sky. She wore the
T-shirt he'd lent her, which thanks to the show she'd
given him a moment ago, he now knew she had
nothing on beneath it. Her shoulders were ramrod
straight, her hands at her sides.

And he had no idea what she was thinking.

"I wanted to spread Blake's ashes into the ocean," she said softly to the window. "Off the bluffs. He would have liked that."

He let out a low breath, knowing what was coming next, hating what was coming next.

"Only there are no ashes."

The pain reverberated in her voice, and somehow bounced off his own chest, rolling over his heart. *Dammit.* He headed toward her.

"All I can do is put a marker next to our parents' graves." Her voice wobbled at this, but she didn't lose it, just stared out at the night. "He's innocent, Aidan."

The Kenzie he'd known had always believed the best of everyone, to a fault. Seemed that hadn't changed, only this time it was going to bite her on the ass.

"And I would have thought you'd think so, too," she said with more than a little accusation in her voice. She sighed, the sound soft and heart-breaking as it shuddered out of her.

"Look," he said. "Why don't you go to bed and get some sleep. You'll feel better if you do."

"I doubt that." But she finally turned from the window. The last of the day's light slanted in through the glass behind her, casting her in its soft glow, rendering the T-shirt just sheer enough to stop his heart.

Not sure how much more of her glorious body he could take without dropping to his knees and begging for mercy, he stayed right where he was instead of getting any closer to her.

Closer would be a mistake, especially with those hugely expressive eyes on his, and that look of grief all over her face.

"Sleep won't change anything that I'm feeling," she whispered. "He'll still be innocent."

"Kenzie, they found a scrapbook of all the fires in Blake's house. He was keeping track of them."

"That doesn't mean he's guilty."

"What *does* it mean?"

"Something else." She hugged herself, looking miserable and alone, and hurting. "I wish we were friends," she said very quietly. "I wish that you hadn't hurt me, and that I didn't have the urge to hurt you back."

Feeling bad, feeling a whole host of things he shouldn't be feeling at all, he took her hand. "I'm sorry I hurt you back then. I'm sorry I let you go. But I was young and stupid, Kenz. I was a complete ass."

She lifted a shoulder, tacitly agreeing with him.

"I'd like to think that if we were seeing each other now," he said softly, "and one of us wanted out, that we'd do better. That we'd make the friendship work."

Another lift of her shoulder, with slightly less temper in it this time.

Okay, that was something, a step at least. Pulling her toward him, he turned to lead her back to his bed, where he was going to tuck her in and then walk away.

Be the good guy.

Only she tugged him back, and suddenly he was holding onto her and she was pressing her face into his throat and breathing in deep, and…and *hell*. He was in trouble, sinking fast. "I showered at the station," he murmured into her hair. "But I need another. I still smell like smoke, Kenz, and—"

"Right." Pulling free, she turned away. "Sorry."

And now she thought he didn't want to hold her, when that was *all* he wanted. "Kenzie—"

"No, you're right. Absolutely right. Let's not go there." She smiled, and anyone who'd ever seen her smile for real would have recognized it as a first-class fake, but he didn't dare say a word about it because he had the feeling she was barely hanging on.

As was he.

She turned away. "You're right. Sleep might be best. But I'll take the couch—"

"No, don't be ridiculous. I—"

"Make no mistake, Aidan. I still want to hurt you. It's immature and extremely juvenile of me, but it's fact. So, no. I'm not sleeping in your bed." She walked back to the couch.

"Kenzie—"

"Please," she said, sinking down to the cushions and closing her eyes. "Could I have a blanket?"

"Of course." He went and got several, came back and spread them over her.

She didn't speak, or for that matter, move.

"Call me if you need anything," he finally said.

She gave no response to that, either, and he nodded even though she wasn't looking at him. "Okay then… night." He paused, but she still didn't say anything to release him from the strange torment he felt. In the end, he did as she seemed to want, and left her alone.

A FEW MINUTES LATER, Kenzie heard the shower go on, and in spite of herself, pictured Aidan stripping off his clothes and climbing in.

Soaping himself up…

Standing there beneath the steamy hot water all naked.

And unintentionally sexy.

Behind her, from somewhere else in the house, a phone rang. A machine clicked on and she heard Aidan's voice saying, "You know what to do at the beep."

Then came a "Hey, you" in a low, Marilyn Monroe–like purr. "It's Lori. You didn't call me back. I've been lonely for you, baby. Come over sometime soon, okay? I'll be waiting…"

Kenzie listened to the click as the machine went off and silence filled the house.

Seemed Aidan was still the guy who left women feeling lonely for him. She should return the favor. She should go…somewhere.

But as she listened to the shower running, she let out a long breath and admitted to herself—as silly as it seemed—there was something undeniably consoling about being here with him. She'd told him she trusted him a little, and that was as truthful as it was unsettling. Yes, she had nowhere else to go, but it was far more than that. At the moment, he was the only familiar, comforting presence in her life. At the moment, she wanted to be there, she really did, even knowing that the longer they spent together, the more they would grow closer, whether she liked it or not.

Only, she was afraid she would like it. A lot more than was wise.

AIDAN SURFACED from a deep, deep sleep, aware that something had woken him, but not sure what. He opened his eyes and saw his dark bedroom lit up in black and white by the faint glow of the moon slanting in through his horizontal blinds.

There, by his bed, stood an angel.

An angel in his T-shirt, in the same white swaths of moonlight as his room.

She was hurting, sad, scared…and why the hell hadn't he given her a suit of armor instead of just a T-shirt? Had he been looking for punishment? Because there it was, in flesh and blood and glorious curves and wild hair, and a face so hauntingly beautiful she took his breath. He was in trouble, deep trouble, because although he'd managed to resist opening his heart to her that first time, he wasn't quite sure he would be able to manage it this time.

Without a single word, she lifted his covers and scooted into the bed.

With him.

He was exhausted, beyond exhausted, and was afraid he didn't have the self-control to deal with this. *"Jesus,"* he gasped as she pressed her icy feet to his.

"Sorry."

But she didn't pull them back. Nope, she tucked them beneath his, sucking the warmth out of him.

"Don't look at me like that," she whispered.

He had no idea what she was talking about. There was no way she could clearly see his expression, she couldn't see any more than he could in the strips of moonlight. He could see her eyes, not her nose. He could see her mouth, not her chin…

"I'm not sleepwalking, or pain-pill walking." She pressed a little closer, so that her legs entangled in his.

Now would probably be as good a time as any to remind her that he slept naked, but as he opened his mouth, she spoke first.

"And I'm not here for another broken heart like I got the last time." She poked a finger into his chest. "In fact, if anyone's going to have a broken heart this time, it's going to be you. So you can just wipe that look of pity off your face."

"Pity is the last thing I've got going on," he assured her. He lay there achingly close, freezing his ass off thanks to her feet. "So you're going to break my heart?"

"Going to do my damnedest."

"I never meant to break yours."

"At least let me think I'm getting my revenge, okay?"

Her toes were killing him. So were her legs, the ones all caught up in his. And somehow he had a thigh between hers…

She propped her head up with her good hand, staring at him in the oddly lit room. Now he could see her forehead and her nose, but not her eyes or her mouth.

"It really is going to be you nursing the heart this time," she whispered.

That could very well be. But honestly, he wasn't sure his bruised heart functioned enough to break. Hell, it was probably dried up from misuse. And yet…and yet lying there with her in his arms seemed to jump-start the organ. It ached, and not just because of their past, it ached for the here and now, for the woman she'd become.

"You," she repeated softly, even a little smugly, and for some reason, some sick reason, it was a turn-on.

And because he was weak and maybe just a little bit stupid, he put his hand on her hip and leaned in to see her better, which he couldn't. She was still in slatted black and white. "I meant what I said, Kenz. I'm sorry you got hurt."

"Good. I *want* you sorry. Very, very sorry."

Yes, but did she want him aroused? Because he was. Her T-shirt had risen up enough to remind him she wasn't wearing panties.

Yeah, colossally stupid.

By now it had to be crystal clear to her that he was butt-ass naked. In the name of fair warning, he pulled her in a little closer.

"What are you doing?"

What was he doing? No idea. Bending his head, he rubbed his jaw to hers, bumped the tip of his nose to her earlobe.

With a shiver, she clutched at him and arched her neck, giving him better access.

Which he took.

"I can't remember what I was saying," she murmured.

He let out a breath in her ear and she shivered again, which he liked. He liked that a lot. "You were telling me how you're going to break my heart."

"That's right." Her fingers dug into the small of his back as she moved, the black and white shadows shifting over her. "I am. Aidan?"

"Yeah?"

"You're naked."

He'd been wondering when that would come up. Seeing as he was already quite "up"…

She gulped, and then did something he didn't expect. She rolled to her back and pulled him on top of her, allowing him to settle between her thighs, which were not cold like her feet, but warm and cushy and very, very welcoming.

"You should know," she whispered in his ear, making sure her lips brushed his flesh, causing a series of shivers of his own. "I plan to make you beg for mercy this time."

*God.* "I'm close to begging right now," he admitted.

"Really?"

She sounded breathless as hell, which was another big turn-on. So many… "Really."

He was hard. She was soft, so soft, and pressing all that softness up against him. "If you're not sleep-walking, or having a bad dream," he wondered, "why are you in here?"

"No hotels, remember?"

"Why are you in bed with me?" he clarified.

Her hands glided up and down his back, going lower on each pass. "My feet were cold."

He pressed his feet to hers, and then his mouth to her throat. "Is that all?"

"Absolutely. That and the begging."

He let out a huff of low laughter against her skin, and then because his mouth was right there against her neck, and because she was touching his butt, and because she smelled good, he took a little nibble.

Her fingers dug into him, telling him how much she liked it but she shook her head. "No more touching until you beg."

"I wasn't touching, I was kissing."

"No kissing until you beg. No anything until you beg."

"I've never begged for this before."

"No? Well, it's good for your character to try new things."

He laughed again. Laughed while trying to get laid. That was new. "Okay." Lifting his head, he cupped her face between his hands and looked into her eyes. She was smiling, too, and it was good to see her doing so. It was good to see her period; his smile slowly faded. "Can I kiss you, Kenzie?"

"Is that the best you got?"

"Can I pretty-please kiss you?"

"Well, I *suppose...*"

That was all he let her get out before he lowered his mouth to hers and kissed her. She let out a little murmur of surprise and what he sincerely hoped was pleasure, because *holy shit,* it was like taking a time machine back in time, back to that sweet, hot, most amazing summer he'd once spent in her arms.

She made the sound again, the one that drove him crazy with wanting, and then she entwined her arms up around his neck, gliding her fingers into his short hair and tightening them, as if she didn't want him going anywhere.

*Fat chance.*

When he slid his tongue to hers, it was another homecoming, and this time her shuddery sigh was pure, hungry delight with a sprinkle of unadulterated lust on top.

*Oh, yeah.* Pulling back just enough to look into her eyes, he found the same sense of bewildered wonderment across her face that he imagined was across his. Because, yes, they were attracted to each other because of their past, but suddenly it was much, much more than that. Then the next thing he knew, they'd lunged for each other again, trying to climb into each other's body, just like old times.

Only it was new, all so damn new, and all the more heart-wrenching and gripping for it. They were no longer young and stupid. They were old enough to know better, old enough to know exactly what they were doing, old enough that he knew that this time, there would be no escaping unscathed.

It didn't stop him.

# 7

OH. MY. GOD.

Kenzie struggled to think, but Aidan had taken her breath away And, as he surged up to his knees between her spread thighs, his hands fisted in the hem of his own shirt, his intention perfectly clear, he nearly stole her sanity—but she held on by a thread. "Wait," she gasped, putting a hand to his chest. "Hold it."

Still kneeling between her sprawled legs, his hands on the big T-shirt, about to strip her as naked as he was, he looked into her eyes. "Wait?"

She could have drowned in his gaze. Happily drowned. "You stopped begging."

He arched an eyebrow, which was highlighted by the slants of moonlight across his face. Stripes of light and dark, and in them, he was beautiful. "I mean it," she managed. "Absolutely nothing else happens here without some serious begging."

He stared at her, then lowered his head for a moment. When he lifted it again, she expected him to tell her he never begged for anything. That this—she— wasn't worth it. After all, she hadn't been once.

But he surprised her. "When we were together," he said quietly, "I dreamed about your body on the nights we didn't sleep in the same bed. Did you know that?"

"No." She shook her head. "You never said." He'd never said a lot of things. He'd held back so much.

*And to be honest, so did I....*

"I'd get off on it," he said, not holding back this time. Which did exactly what she hadn't wanted—it opened her heart to him.

"On you," he murmured. "For years afterward, I'd get off thinking about you."

She stared up at him. "You mean you..."

"Uh-huh. I jerked off." Leaning over her, he was nothing but a shadow until he bent even closer. Through the shutters, rectangles of light slashed over him as he let her look into his eyes, which were dark and scorching. "So much I'm lucky I'm not blind."

She laughed but also swallowed hard, surprisingly aroused at the thought of his touching himself while picturing her. "Oh."

"Yeah, oh." His eyes glittered with heat and memories and suddenly both the heat and memories were making her feel awfully warm from the inside out.

Actually, they were making her hot.

Very hot.

"Tonight, just looking at you..." He let out a long breath and shook his head. "It brings it all back, but it's even stronger."

His mouth was in the shadows. She couldn't see his lips moving but his voice washed over her, as did the images he evoked. He was bringing it all back for her, too.

"You were beautiful then," he said. "But you're even more beautiful now. I want to take this shirt off of you, Kenz. Please let me."

At his words, she nearly turned the tables and begged *him*. She could feel the T-shirt caught high on her thighs. His hips were holding her legs open to him, and with just a little nudge of the shirt, he'd be able to see all her god-given goodies, along with the fact that she was already wet.

"Please," he murmured. "Please let me."

*Oh, God.* "Yes."

He shifted, and then she could see his mouth, which rewarded her with a smile as he made his move, his fingers closing around the hem of the shirt, slowly tugging it up, revealing her body.

She'd wanted this, sought it out under the guise of getting her long-needed revenge, but that was really just a lie, and her first flicker of doubt hit.

*Just who was going to get hurt here…?*

The night air brushed over her breasts as he pulled the shirt all the way off and over her head. Her nipples hardened. Goose bumps spread over her flesh, and it wasn't because she was cold. There were five stripes of moonlight across her body, one across her eyes, her throat, another highlighting her breasts, her belly and her crotch. He couldn't have lined her up more perfectly for his perusal, and he definitely perused.

"Aidan—"

His hand stroked over her hip, and her breath backed up into her throat. She opened her mouth to say maybe she'd been hasty about this whole breaking his heart thing, but before she could, he'd put a hand on her inner thigh and pushed, further opening her to him.

The slants of shadows hampered his view, but he didn't seem bothered, not with his front row seat.

The only sound in the room came from him as he let out a groan. "God, Kenzie. You're so pretty." He lowered his head, then paused, his mouth a hairsbreadth away from her trembling belly. "I want to kiss. I want to taste. I want that more than I want my next breath. Please let me…"

As far as begging went, it was pretty good. "O-okay," she managed, and almost before the word was out, he'd nudged her legs open even wider, wedging them there with his broad shoulders. He slowly lowered his head. "Pretty please," he whispered across her flesh.

Her wet flesh.

*"Yes."* Her heels dug into the mattress as he "pretty pleased" his tongue over her, and then his teeth, and then his warm lips, over and over again leaving her a panting, gasping, quivery mass of sensitized nerve endings, and when she exploded for him, he surged up, produced a condom and slid into her with one sure, powerful thrust.

"Oh," she gasped, reaching up to hold onto him because her world had just spun on its axis. The feel of him deep inside her—and he was deep, as deep as he could get—had her spiraling. Gone were all thoughts of hurting him, or revenge. She could think of nothing but this, but him. Not that she would admit such a thing. "You…you didn't beg for that."

Cupping her face, he tilted it up to his. "Pretty-please may I drive you out of your living mind?"

*Oh, God.*

"Kenzie? May I?" His voice was thick with the same hunger and need that was driving her.

"Yes."

"Good. May I also pretty-please make you scream my name?"

In answer, she arched up, her breasts pressing into his hard, warm chest, her legs wrapping around his waist.

He groaned, a low, rough sound that scraped at all her good spots but he didn't move. "Can I?"

"I don't usually do much screaming."

He just smiled, and then took her mouth as he took her body, indeed driving her out of her mind with all too disturbing ease, and when she exploded again, she cried out his name.

Loudly.

She might have even screamed it.

As the blood finally slowed in her veins, as the roar of it lowered to a trickle in her head, she became aware of the fact that she was gripping him tight, holding him close with her arms and her legs, not letting him escape.

He didn't say a word, just nuzzled lazily at her neck as his breathing slowed.

Hers wasn't slowing. Embarrassed at how tightly

she was holding him, she forced herself to let him go, certain he'd roll away.

But in perhaps the loveliest thing he'd done all night, he didn't. Instead, he remained right where he was, turning just his head to press his lips to her jaw, murmuring her name on a sigh.

It was one of those defining moments, where she suddenly knew the truth—she'd not exacted a single ounce of revenge. In fact, she'd made things worse.

She'd risked her own heart.

But for that one moment at least, she didn't care, because maybe he'd changed. Maybe things could be different this time, and—

"You screamed my name." He lifted his head, revealing a strong smile. "You begged." He out-and-out grinned then, not broken, not even a little bit. "We still work hard."

"There's no *we*." She pushed him off her, suddenly and irrationally irritated. "No we at all."

Completely oblivious to the picture he made sprawled out on the bed, buck naked, he put his hands behind his head and continued to smile like an idiot. "Are you telling me you have no desire to do that again?"

"None."

"Ah, Kenzie. You're such a pretty liar."

*Yeah.* Yeah, she was. A pretty liar, and a good liar. But she had no idea how else to hide the fact that she still had feelings for him in spite of their past—or maybe because of it. *God.* She needed to get out for a while, needed to clear her head. Get some answers. *Alone.*

"Stay," he murmured.

"Okay." She looked at him. "I'll stay if you tell me this. Why did you really dump me?"

At that, his amusement faded. "I told you I was an idiot back then."

"Granted. Why else?"

He looked at her and she nearly backed down; she certainly held her breath, but he touched her face. "Because I didn't know what I had."

AIDAN SLEPT like the dead. Or like a man who'd been far too close to serious exhaustion. When he opened his eyes, he felt the various aches and pains from the fire, and from the mattress gymnastics he and Kenzie had executed, and was grateful to know he had two days off, because more sleep was on his To Do list. Much more.

So was more mattress gymnastics.

Considering that Kenzie was wrapped around him like a pretzel, that shouldn't be too difficult to manage. As he looked into her face, taking in each of the cuts and the bruises there in the light of day, he felt a tug in his belly.

He wished like hell he could say he was just hungry, but he knew the truth.

He was a goner.

She was as cut up and bruised as he was, more so, and if *he* hurt like hell, he could only imagine how she felt. He was used to such injuries. She wasn't.

"I realize I've spent my days on a television set,

where my worst injury was a paper cut from that day's script," she whispered, eyes still closed. "But I'm not feeling as bad as I probably look."

Her face was relaxed now; and he realized it hadn't been before—not on Blake's boat, not when she'd crawled in bed with him, not even when he'd stripped her out of his shirt and proceeded to make her scream.

That he'd undone her so easily didn't stroke his ego. She'd undone him just the same. It'd always been like that for them, a virtual explosion of need and lust and hunger.

But he'd attributed much of that to being young and horny. He hadn't anticipated a resurgence of those feelings, And he doubted she had either. But that's exactly what they'd gotten.

With a sigh, she slid out of his arms and off the bed. He enjoyed the view as she walked to the bathroom, but when she shut the door, his smile faded. She needed sustenance, and a bandage change. Getting up, he pulled on his jeans and went into the kitchen, where he grabbed a pan and eggs and went to work getting them both some protein so that they could go back to bed and burn it all off again.

His doorbell rang and Aidan stopped dicing peppers long enough to sign the clipboard of a pudgy guy in brown shorts, who handed him a slim package.

When he heard the shower go off, he finished the eggs and then grabbed his first-aid bag and knocked on the door. "Bandages, aspirin and breakfast. And your package from L.A. is here."

"Perfect timing—I've got to run."

"You mean back to Los Angeles?"

The door opened and steam came out. As did Kenzie wrapped in another of his towels. "Not back. Not yet."

The towel was tucked between her breasts, which pushed them up and nearly out, a fact he'd have taken the time to thoroughly enjoy except for the nasty bruise arcing along her left collar bone. "You need rest."

"I need clothes." She moved past him and into his bedroom. "Can I borrow a pair of sweats?"

"Sure." He opened his dresser and handed the clothes over.

"Thanks. I've really got to go."

She was going to go snoop. Get in Tommy's way. Get herself arrested. "Kenzie, listen to me. You need to stay out of the investigation. The chief doesn't want you digging—"

"I don't work for him. He can't tell me what to do."

"If you stay—"

"No. Thank you, but, no."

Usually in the light of day, with a woman in his bedroom, *he* was the one who had to go. Usually.

Okay, always.

It felt odd to have the shoe on the other foot. Especially given the magnitude of what they'd shared last night, and he wasn't alone in feeling it, dammit. He knew he wasn't.

But Kenzie moved carefully away from him, slowly, as if still in pain, but with conviction. She was set on going, leaving him with a disconcerted feeling in his gut.

Was this how he'd made women feel? Like they'd

already been forgotten? "Let's change your bandages—"

"I can do it on my own."

Seemed she was used to doing stuff on her own. That was new.

So was his unsettledness over the way this was going down.

"Yeah," she said at his quiet surprise. "I'm not the same helpless little thing I used to be."

"I never thought you were helpless."

"Well, I was. But I've grown up. I've changed. In many ways. And I don't need anyone's help. For anything."

He arched an eyebrow. "You needed me when we—"

"No. Well, yes, *yes,* I needed you to save me from the fire, but—"

"That's not what I was talking about." He pointed to his bed.

"Oh, no. That was just me, breaking your heart. I warned you, remember."

Bullshit. That hadn't been just revenge. "Kenzie."

"Sorry. Got to go. Have to go." Once again she dropped her towel, which had the same magical effect on him as it had last night. While he stood there taking in the glorious sight of her naked body, she pulled on the sweats, kissed him on the cheek, then walked out of the room.

And, given the sound of the front door opening and then closing, out of his house.

And, most likely, out of his life.

Fitting justice really, as he'd once done the same to her. Moving to the living room, he looked out the window in time to catch her taillights as they vanished down his driveway.

*I've changed,* she'd said, and she had.

But as the blood once again began a northward flow from behind the zipper of his pants back up to his brain, another thought managed to get his attention.

He'd changed as well. And he was going to prove it.

# 8

SOMEONE WAS KNOCKING on Aidan's door when he turned off the shower. *She'd come back.* With his pulse kicking, he grabbed a towel and wrapped it around his waist, heading for the door at a speed far faster than his usual get-there-when-I-get-there saunter.

Only it wasn't Kenzie at all. "Dammit."

His best friend and partner Zach just looked at him. "Nice to see you, too." Without waiting for an invitation, he pushed past Aidan and walked in.

Fair enough. Aidan had let himself into Zach's house plenty of times. Aidan shut the door behind Zach and shoved his fingers through his wet hair. "Sorry. Thought you were someone else."

Zach took in Aidan standing there dripping wet, wearing only a towel. "Clearly. Who is she?"

"How do you know it's a she?"

"Because if you're meeting a guy dressed like that, we have a whole different issue to talk about."

Aidan rolled his eyes and left Zach to go get some clothes. In his bedroom, he looked at his bed as he pulled on a clean shirt. The covers were tossed half on the floor, and on his nightstand were two empty condom wrappers.

And though it was crazy given that Kenzie had used his shampoo, his clothes and his soap, he'd have sworn he could smell her scent, some complicated mix of soft, determined, sexy woman. He stared at the bed, remembering how he'd felt when she'd crawled in with him, remembering how natural it'd been to kiss and touch her, to sink into her body and go to a place he hadn't been in a long time.

Then they'd slept together, and that had felt good, too, being all tangled up in each other again. Familiar, but new. Even better, if that was possible. Things hadn't been complicated in the dark.

Things had been amazing.

But she'd left.

When he walked back into the kitchen, he found Zach staring at the breakfast he'd made for Kenzie.

"You made breakfast," Zach said. "As in got out a pan and cooked something."

"Yeah. So?"

"You put out napkins."

"Let me repeat myself. So?"

"So you never put out napkins. Not when it's me or the other guys."

"Do you want to split the food with me or not?"

"You didn't cook this for me."

"You're right."

Zach raised an eyebrow.

"You're going to question a plate of food?" Aidan said. "Really?"

Zach didn't have to be asked twice. He grabbed a plate and pulled up a chair.

"I thought you and Brooke were going away for a few days since you haven't been cleared to go back to work yet."

"We are. We're leaving tomorrow morning. Wanted to see you first."

"Ah, that's so sweet. You're going to miss me."

"Actually, I'm not." Zach shoveled in some food, and looked at him. "I heard about the explosion. I should have been there."

Aidan looked at the cast on Zach's left wrist, remembered how close he'd come to losing him along with Blake, and felt the food get caught in his throat. "You're not healed yet."

"It's coming along though." He squeezed his fingers into a fist, then stretched them straight out. "I could be back at work, dammit. I have no idea why the chief's being so hard-assed about this. I'm willing and able."

"Enjoy your few days off. You and Brooke deserve it."

"Yeah." Zach sighed. "So is the boat a complete loss?"

"Unfortunately."

"Kenzie all right?"

"Heard about that, too, huh?"

"Yeah." Zach paused. "Was it awkward, considering your past with her?"

"To be the one rescuing her?"

"What else?"

*Yeah, genius, what else.* Maybe sleeping with her… But that hadn't been awkward. Not one little bit.

Zach was looking at him. "What am I missing?"

Aidan shook his head. "Nothing."

"Come on."

"Okay, nothing I want to talk about."

"That I buy," Zach said, and like the good friend he was, changed the subject. "I heard that Blake must have kept his accelerants on the boat, which is why it blew like it did."

That was one theory, Aidan was sure.

But he had another. "Well…"

"What?" Zach asked.

"You're going to tell me I'm crazy."

Zach stood up and went to the refrigerator for the milk. "All those times I thought those fires were arson, you were the only one who believed me. I'll be the last one to tell you that you're crazy."

"Yeah, but now we know that Tommy was behind you the entire time, he was just in the middle of his investigation. Still is, with the chief riding his ass to put an end to this."

"Yeah." Zach pushed away his plate. "So I wonder what they'd say now."

"About…?"

"About your not buying that boat fire was any more accidental than the other fires. Or me not buying it, either."

Aidan looked into his best friend's eyes and let out a breath. "That boat was blown up for a reason and I think that reason was to hide something. Something that someone didn't want found."

"What?"

"I don't know. And I'm betting Tommy and the Chief don't know either but they want to."

"It doesn't make sense," Zach said. "Blake's dead."

Aidan pushed away his plate. "Yeah." Goddamn, but he wasn't going to get used to that any time soon, the fact that Blake, a friend, *one of them* for Christ's sake, was not only gone, but accused of arson. "Which means that he wasn't working alone and whoever the other person is, they're running scared of something."

"Or someone," Zach said. "Kenzie shows up out of the blue after what, six years? Seems kind of odd, doesn't it?"

Aidan's gut tightened. "Her brother's dead, Zach."

"Yes. Her arsonist brother. They were close, right?"

"What are you saying, that she's his co-felon?"

"Look, I don't want to think about Blake doing the things they've accused him of, either. And I really don't want to think about the fact that if he was still alive, he'd be in jail. But those are the facts."

Aidan scrubbed his hands over his face. "She *just* got into town."

"You know that for sure?"

Actually, no, he didn't.

"Why was she on his boat?"

"Going through his things." Listen to him defend her. "Missing him."

Zach closed his eyes and rubbed them hard. "If that were true, wouldn't she have come sooner?"

"I don't know. I don't know anything except that Blake was all she had." Aidan got to his feet because he had to move, had to pace the length of the kitchen. "She's…devastated. Horrified. And pissed off that we all believe that Blake's guilty. I think she's going to go digging on her own and find out what she can."

"Which should make Tommy oh-so-happy."

"He's going to have her arrested if she hinders the investigation," Aidan admitted. "And she's going to hinder. It's in her nature. She intends to prove Blake innocent."

Zach raised a brow. "You got all that from pulling her out of the water?"

*Well, shit.* Aidan picked up his fork and shoveled some food in.

"You saw her after the fire. At the hospital."

"Yeah."

Zach paused. "And after that as well, I'm thinking."

"Yeah."

Zach peered around Aidan and into the living room, pointedly looking down the hallway.

"She's not still here."

"But she *was* here? Jesus, Aidan. What would Tommy say?"

"Since when does that matter?"

"Since we both now know that he was on our side about the arsons all along. He'll be on this, too, you can guarantee it."

Yeah. In hindsight, sleeping with Kenzie been a pretty stupid thing to do. And yet, what else could he have done but given her a place to stay?

Except for that using up two condoms part. He probably could have not done that.

"We've got to let Tommy do his thing here," Zach said quietly.

"I can't believe you're suggesting I stay out of it, when you did the very opposite."

"And paid for it," Zach reminded him, lifting his casted wrist.

"She was hurting, Zach. And alone. Her purse had burned in the fire and she had nowhere else to go so I let her stay here. End of story."

"You could have lent her money. She's a famous soap diva—I think she'd have been good for it."

"The hotels were all booked up."

When Zach just looked at him, Aidan lifted a shoulder. "It was just bad luck on her part."

"Just bad luck, huh? Funny, you don't look so put out."

"Don't you have a fiancée to go home to?"

Zach grinned dopily. "Yeah."

"So go already."

Zach got up, then paused. "Look, Aidan, I know she meant something to you once, but—"

"She's Blake's sister."

"And *your* ex. I'd think that'd be reason enough to stay away from her."

*Yeah.* One would think…

OPENING THE SLIM ENVELOPE she'd scooped from Aidan's kitchen table on her way out the door, Kenzie practically kissed the credit card she found inside. She needed some personal items, like clothes of her own, not to mention underwear. Not that she didn't love Aidan's sweats, because she did. They smelled like him. They felt like him.

Which was exactly why she had to get *out* of them.

She did her best not to pout over the loss of her Choos, which she wasn't going to find at Wal-Mart, but the store was still one of God's greatest creations. When she'd bought and put on a peasant skirt, two layered tank tops and a pair of sandals, she got back into her car. She'd missed two calls on her cell, both from that same local number as before, but no messages, so she put it out of her head and drove to the docks. Then she sat in the parking lot nursing a hot chocolate and a blessed box of donuts, staring at the charred remains of Blake's boat.

She was alone except for the occasional car. One was a light-gray sedan that slowed as it passed her, the windows so dark that she couldn't see in. Probably another looky-loo like herself, except…except she'd seen a car like it before, somewhere…

She ate a donut.

Until a couple of weeks ago, before Blake's death, she hadn't had chocolate or donuts in months. Maybe years. She'd been on a strict eighteen-hundred-calorie diet, combined with a workout every single day, without fail. All to look good.

That's what TV stars did. They looked good. She was paid to.

Except she no longer had a TV show to look good for. Back in L.A., she knew the job-finding frenzy had already begun. All her co-stars were busy auditioning, and what was she doing? Eating donuts instead of facing the fact that she was unemployed.

Her cushy, easy, comfortable, fun job had come to an end.

Life over.

She looked at *Blake's Girl* and felt the last donut congeal in her throat. No. Her job was over, not her life.

*Blake's* life was over.

*God.* Brushing the sugar from her fingers, she got out of the car. She wasn't looking her best, but then again, there were no paparazzi in Santa Rey. And thanks to no one in the press making the connection between her and *Blake's Girl,* there were no reporters to take pics of her pale, makeup-free face, or all of the bruises and cuts she'd sustained in the fire. Her wrist wasn't bothering her, but the splint was a pain in the butt. She hadn't been able to corral her hair into a ponytail, which meant it was flying wild around her face and in her eyes.

She could have asked Aidan for help but she'd rather have the wild hair than have his hands on her again.

Okay, that wasn't true, wasn't anywhere close to true, but she could pretend it was.

*Dammit.*

For those few hours last night in his arms, she'd not

been alone and lost and hurting. She'd been transported, taken out of herself.

And along the way, she'd forgotten to make him regret dumping her. *Nicely done.* Rolling her eyes at herself, she moved closer to the docks. The charred remains of *Blake's Girl* were taped off with yellow crime scene tape.

She didn't know what that was about.

They thought Blake was a criminal? Fine. But they couldn't pin this one on him, he was already gone.

Gone...

Chest tight, she walked along the yellow tape, getting as close as she could, which wasn't close enough. No one was around, on the dock or otherwise, and she couldn't stop the thought—what if she ducked under the tape? Surely, as Blake's only living relative, she deserved to have a look.

The two boats on either side of *Blake's Girl* were still there. Barely. One was nearly burned black, and in fact looked as if it might still be steaming. The other was half gone, and half untouched.

And between them? A shell of a boat, blackened and charred beyond recognition.

Blake's boat was completely destroyed.

Looking at it, she could see it as it'd been two nights ago, when she could stand on it and still feel her brother's presence, when his things had still been okay. She wished she'd gotten something of his, something, anything...

Maybe she could crawl beneath the tape and get onboard to comb through the torched remains, and thinking it, she bent down, but at the sound of an engine, stopped and turned.

It was the gray sedan again, making another pass of the parking lot.

Goose bumps rose on her arms as she got that same sensation of being watched she'd had at the hospital.

Who was following her?

It wasn't Aidan. No way. He'd make himself known, that was for damn sure. He had a way of making himself known…

Someone else then.

Tommy?

No. Tommy didn't have the resources to have her followed. She doubted anyone in Santa Rey did.

Then she remembered her earlier missed calls, and pulled out her phone, hitting the number.

No one answered.

She ran her hand along the yellow police tape, but the truth was, she didn't quite have the nerve to boldly defy the law.

At least not during the daylight hours.

But tonight…

Yeah, tonight.

Under the cover of darkness.

Turning away, she squeaked as she accidentally bumped into a hard wall.

A hard wall that was really a warm, hard chest she recognized all too well, along with the big, warm hands that settled on her arms.

# 9

THE COLLISION SET KENZIE back a step, but Aidan held her upright.

She tilted her head up, up, up…and looked into his face, which was unfortunately indecipherable.

"You okay?" he asked, his voice low and calm, and concerned.

Okay, concern was good. Concern implied that he hadn't noticed what she'd been about to do. But was she okay? *Hell, no.*

Not even close.

"Are you?" His gaze swept down her body, then up again, as if categorizing her injuries, which reminded her of last night, when he'd also been categorized her body.

With his tongue.

"Yes," she managed. "I'm fine."

"Good. What the hell are you doing here?"

"Funny, I was going to ask you the same thing. Are you following me?"

"No."

"You're not driving a gray sedan and going everywhere I go?"

"I drive a truck, a blue one and I didn't follow you here. I got lucky on the first try. I figured you'd come here and try to do something stupid."

"I did nothing of the kind."

"You don't consider ducking beneath that yellow tape stupid?"

"Only if I'd gotten caught."

"Hello," he said, still holding on to her. His fingers tightened. *"Caught."*

"Yes, but you don't count."

He looked both boggled *and* irritated. "And why is that?"

"Because what are you going to do, arrest me? Last night you were kissing me, touching me, fu—"

"Okay," he said with a low laugh. "Now just hold on a second—"

"I'm just saying." She narrowed her eyes and went for bravado, even though she could hardly breathe while looking at the big blackened sailboat that less than two days ago had been *Blake's Girl*.

Aidan had saved her.

He'd saved her and she was poking at him because she was all twisted up inside. So she let out a breath and looked into his face, where she found a surprising blend of sympathy and old affection mixed in with the frustration and fear.

"I came here to talk," he said. "Not arrest you. Jesus. Now what the hell is this about a gray sedan?"

"Nothing."

He just looked at her for a long moment. "What aren't you telling me?"

"Nothing."

"More like everything." He let out a breath. "Tommy expects you to let him do his job."

"I'm not going to get in his way. I'm going to help him."

"Now see, I don't think he likes help."

"Too bad for him."

"It's going to be too bad for you if you piss him off. He can and will have you arrested if you don't stay out of his way."

"Believe me, I plan to stay out of his way."

"Okay." He nodded. "New subject then."

*Uh-oh.*

"Last night…"

Kenzie didn't know how she felt about last night. And because she didn't, she absolutely didn't want to talk about it. "Yeah. Now's not a good time for me."

"You don't think so?"

She shook her head.

His eyes lit with something that might have been wry humor. He'd been just as beat up as her yesterday, but unlike her, today he did not look like something the cat dragged in. No, he looked tall and fit, and in his loose cargoes and T-shirt, he seemed very in charge of himself and his world.

She, on the other hand, was in charge of exactly nothing at the moment. "Maybe later." And maybe not.

He hadn't taken his hands off of her arms, and if

asked she'd have said she wasn't sure how she felt about that, but that would be a lie. At the moment, his support felt like a lifeline.

Her only lifeline. "Tell me something," she said very quietly, her eyes on his so she didn't miss any little nuance, because this was very, very important to her. "Arson. It's a well studied crime, right? The people who do it, most of them belong to a particular character type. Aggressive. Violent. Repeat offenders."

"Yes," he agreed. "How do you know this?"

"We did a whole plotline about an arsonist last year. Would you characterize Blake as aggressive or violent?"

"Not even close."

"Exactly," she said.

"Which doesn't prove anything. There's physical evidence—"

"Okay," she agreed. She knew about the evidence. "But most arsonists *want* their work admired. Isn't that correct?"

"Yes, but—"

"*But* Blake maintained his innocence. Tommy told me that much."

"Yes," Aidan agreed, his expression reflecting his worry for her, whether he wanted it to or not.

Which she didn't want to face. She meant to do two things when it came to Aidan, especially after last night. First: keep her distance. And second: leave *him* pining for *her*.

It was going to be nearly impossible to handle the second while doing the first but she would give it her best shot. "So can't you concede that it's possible that you're wrong about Blake?"

"I'm not the one accusing him of anything."

She looked at him, really looked at him, and understood something she'd missed before. He didn't want to believe the worst of Blake any more than she did, and that was so much more than she expected from him, from anyone, that it was like a balm to all her fear and grief.

He wasn't against her or Blake. She wasn't completely alone, at least not in that moment, and she found herself closing the gap between them to wrap her arms around his broad shoulders, hugging him hard, so damn relieved to have him there with her.

With a rough sound, his arms came around her, too, and he pulled her in, letting her lean on him. "Kenzie," he whispered, bowing his head over hers. "It's okay. It's going to be okay."

*Yeah.* Keeping her distance from him was going to be damned tough.

So would be breaking his heart, but she was still going to do it. It was that, or see hers crushed again, and that was simply not going to happen.

Aidan had never been a hugging sort of guy. He loved physical contact, especially the naked kind, with the fairer sex, but touching just out of sheer affection and nothing else? That hadn't really been a part of his life. Having been the sort of child who'd made it difficult for others to like him, much less love him, he hadn't inspired a lot of affection growing up. And working with mostly guys all the time…well, they tended to shove and wrestle rather than hug.

So this, with Kenzie, should have felt awkward. Alien. At the very least it was an intrusion of his personal space that he would have thought would make him squirm to be free.

But it didn't. Even though a piece of her hair was poking him in the eye and she was stepping on his toe, and her nose—pressed against his throat—was icy enough to make him wince, he didn't move.

In fact, he tightened his arms on her, pressing his face into her hair, inhaling her as if he didn't want to let go.

Because he really didn't.

She was warm and soft and sweet, and when her fingers slid into his hair he nearly purred. His hand skimmed down her spine, pressing low on her back, urging her even closer as he just continued to breathe her in.

Just down the dock, two seagulls argued over some found treasure. Water slapped at the wood pylons. Beyond that, the devastation of the fire sat right before their eyes. Aidan didn't want her looking at it. "You need to get out of here."

"Yeah." She stepped back. "I know. I'm going."

He caught her hand, and when she looked at him questioningly, he saw the truth in her eyes. Wherever she was headed, it was to make trouble.

"I'm a big girl now."

*Yes.* She was a woman who could more than take

care of herself. Which in no way eradicated the need within him to protect her. "Have you eaten?"

She stared at him, then let out a low breath. "I tell you I can take care of myself and you want to feed me? Even after I also told you that I only wanted to be with you in order to break your heart?"

"Yeah, see, about that…" He stroked a loose strand of hair off her face, letting his finger trace the rim of her ear, absorbing her little shiver. "I don't really believe you."

"Oh, it's true," she said with utter conviction. "I'm going to break your heart."

"That wasn't the only reason you stayed with me last night. Slept with me."

"Okay, true. You saved my life. I owed you."

He shook his head. "That wasn't it, either."

"What was it then, smart guy?"

"You like being with me."

A helpless laugh escaped her at that.

"I like being with you, too, Kenz."

She shook her head. "You're off your rocker."

"Already established. So. Food?"

She stared at him, then caved. "I guess I could eat."

She followed him in her car to Sunrise Café. Aidan had no idea why he took her there, other than that taking her back to his place, where they'd be alone, seemed like a really bad idea.

Sheila was thrilled to see him and gave him a huge hug, smiling with some speculation at Kenzie. Even though it was afternoon by then, Aidan ordered a large breakfast. When Kenzie tried to get just coffee, he merely doubled his order, and then took her up to the roof.

There was a long bench against the far wall, where they sat to watch the surf. It was rough, which didn't stop the surfers from enjoying it.

Kenzie stared out at the waves. "It's nice up here. A good place to think. You come here a lot?"

"I do."

"Sheila's fond of you."

"Very," he agreed.

She smiled at him, and just like that, melted his heart. "You've made some good ties," she said softly.

He got a little lost in her eyes, and leaned in with some half-baked idea of kissing her, and—

*"Come and get it!"* Sheila yelled up from the bottom of the stairwell.

Sighing—what else could he do—Aidan led the way down to the crowded dining room. Sheila seated them, then brought them their plates, winking at Aidan before leaving.

Kenzie looked down at her loaded plate. "I'm not that hungry."

"Uh-huh." He nudged her fork closer to her fingers. "That's what you always used to say. You'd tell me you weren't hungry and then you'd eat everything off my plate, remember?"

Humor lit her eyes. "What I remember is that you were my boyfriend. You were supposed to share."

"So, what are you saying? That you wouldn't, say, eat off Chad's plate?"

"Chase. And he's vegan and doesn't eat anything that isn't completely raw, so, no, I wouldn't."

Aidan leaned over and stroked another stray strand of hair off her cheek. He had no idea why he kept finding excuses to touch her, other than she looked sad and just a little lost. She wore no makeup, and all those gorgeous blond waves had rioted around her face, a few long strands curling around her jaw. It was just Kenzie. No smoke and mirrors, no pomp or celebrity. Just the woman who'd once touched his heart.

And, apparently, still did.

So he did what he'd wanted to do on the roof—he leaned over their food and kissed her, just once, softly on the lips. When he pulled back, she gave a baffled little smile and touched her fingers to her mouth. "What was that for?"

Before he could answer, Zach walked up to their table. "Hey."

"Hey," Aidan said in surprise. "Kenzie, this is Zach. Zach, Kenzie is—"

"Blake's sister." Zach's eyes softened as he looked at her. "I miss your brother."

"Thank you," she murmured. "Me, too."

Zach turned to Aidan and handed him a file.

"What's this?"

"I wanted you to have it while I was gone. In case you need it for anything."

Aidan opened the file and instantly knew what he held. All the evidence Zach had gathered over the past few months on the mysterious arsons. Zach had been the first one to suspect something was going on and the first to go to Tommy for answers. Closing the file he met Zach's steady gaze. "Thanks. Want to join us?"

"Can't. Brooke's waiting for me. I just talked to Eddie and Sam. Did you know there was another explosion last night? The hardware store on Sixth."

"Injuries?"

"Several, and one death. Tracy Gibson."

Aidan's stomach dropped. The woman Blake had had a crush on for months before his death.

Kenzie divided her gaze between them. "Who's Tracy?"

"She was an employee at the hardware store," Zach told her. "Same setup as *Blake's Girl,*" he said to Aidan, tapping the file with meaning. "So keep this."

Aidan understood. Zach thought he might need the info in the file when he was gone.

"Nice meeting you," Zach said to Kenzie. With a squeeze to Aidan's shoulder, he left.

"So what does that mean?" Kenzie asked. "If there was a similar explosion, maybe Blake's boat wasn't an accident."

"Maybe."

"A new serial arsonist?" she scoffed. "What are the chances of that in a small town like this?"

"I don't know."

"I know," she said. "Next to nil."

She was watching him with sadness still in her eyes, along with a sense of sharp intelligence that said she wasn't going to let this go. The brash tilt of her chin alluded to a strength of will, of passion, he knew first-hand, and suddenly he was afraid for her.

For her, *of her,* and of the feelings she invoked inside him. Damn, not again... Not falling for her again, he told himself. But it didn't matter that he was seated across from her in a crowded café, surrounded by people.

She was all he saw.

He watched her push her food around the plate for a few minutes, then wrapped his fingers around her wrist, guiding her fork to a large bite of eggs and bringing it to her mouth.

She took it into her mouth, chewed and swallowed, all with her gaze never leaving his. "You keep looking at me like you care."

"I do."

"You shouldn't."

"Why not?"

"Because I'm not going to care about you back." At that, she broke eye contract and stared down at the food. "At least not like I did before."

"So you've mentioned."

"I mean it."

"I believe you." He also believed that she just might get her big wish, because looking at her sitting there, knowing *she'd* be walking away from *him* this time, caused a strange sensation deep inside him. He'd have sworn it was his heart rolling over and exposing its underbelly.

Kenzie took another bite of food as his cell phone

buzzed. It was Dispatch. "Sorry," he said, standing. "I have to take this."

"No problem." She was suddenly engrossed in her food, not even looking up when he went outside to get good enough reception to hear that two firefighters had come down with the flu. They needed replacements for the next shift. So much for a day off—he was going back on duty, starting now.

He turned to go back inside the café and nearly bumped into Kenzie. "Sorry," she said, flashing a smile that didn't quite meet her eyes. "I've got to go."

*Huh.* That had been *his* line.

"I paid the bill—"

He reached for his wallet. "Let me—"

But she put her hand over his and shook her head. "It's on me. Consider it a very small down payment."

"For what?"

"For what I owe you for saving my life."

"Kenzie—"

"Thank you," she said softly, looking into his eyes, making his head spin. "I'm not sure I said that enough. I am extremely grateful."

Wait. That sounded like a good-bye. "Okay, hold on a second. Are you—"

Going up on tiptoes, she put a hand to his chest, leaned in and kissed him on the jaw. She added a smile to the mix, one that went all the way to her eyes this time as she touched her fingers to her lips and then blew him another kiss.

Then she turned and walked away.

As he'd once done to her. "Kenzie."

But she'd already gotten into her car. Where the hell was she going? She revved the engine and was gone, out of the lot, perhaps out of his world. He stood there a moment, absorbing a barrage of emotions, starting with regret and ending with a surprising hurt, and then he shrugged it off and walked inside to say good-bye to Sheila. That's when his head stopped spinning and it hit him.

Kenzie had stolen his file.

# *10*

UNFORTUNATELY FOR KENZIE, the doggie convention was still in town. She tried a couple of B and Bs and got excited when a cute front desk clerk recognized her and said he'd stir up a room. But then he picked up his phone and yelled, "Ma! Get out of the room, I've got a girl!"

Kenzie shouldn't have been surprised, since her karma was clearly still on vacation. She made the clerk leave his mother in the room and escaped. Back in her car, she sighed, feeling very alone.

She missed Blake.

And dammit, she already missed Aidan, too. Missed his voice, his smile, his touch.

How was that even possible? She'd just left him. She'd stolen his file for God's sake. No doubt he was cursing her right this minute.

And definitely *not* missing her.

She pulled into the library and made herself comfortable on a large chair in a far corner, then opened the file. Almost immediately she felt an odd prickle of awareness, and then the hair on the back of her neck stood up.

She was being watched again.

She craned her neck left and then right, but no one in her immediate area was so much as looking at her. Behind her was a set of shelves, and she shifted, trying to see through a gap to the aisle on the other side.

Nothing.

Clearly she was still in the process of losing her mind. Determined, she went back to the file. Zach and Aidan had been thorough. There was a list of fire calls from Firehouse Thirty-Four over the past six months, five of them highlighted. The questionable fires, she realized.

The arsons Blake had ultimately been accused of starting.

Attached were details of those five properties: architectural plans, permits, a history of ownership, purchases and sales. Each had been plotted out on a map, and scrutinized up one side and down the other, including everything that had been found on site after the fire.

Zach had noted finding a metal mesh trash can at each site, and even had a picture of one, from the fire just before the one at Zach's own house. As she was looking at it, her cell phone vibrated. She nearly ignored it until she saw it was the same local cell phone number as before, and she grabbed it. "Hello?" she said breathlessly.

When several people in chairs nearby glared at her, especially one older woman going through a stack of history books, Kenzie hunched her shoulders, mouthed a "sorry" and whispered "hello" much more softly.

An equally soft voice spoke in return. "Forget about it, forget about *all* of it, and go back to Los Angeles."

Kenzie clutched the phone. She couldn't tell if she recognized the speaker because the voice was purposely being disguised. "Is that a threat?"

"You're going to be stubborn. Goddammit."

*"Who is this?"* she demanded.

"It doesn't matter. Just get the hell out of Santa Rey."

"So you *are* threatening me."

"If I said yes, would you go?"

"No."

*"Shit."* There was a beat of silence. "Okay, listen to me. There's only one way out of this."

*"What?"* she said, forgetting to whisper, receiving more glares for that. With effort, she lowered her voice. "What do you mean?"

"Your laptop was destroyed in the boat fire?"

"How do you know that?"

"You have backup."

"What does that have to do with—" She went still as it hit her. She and Blake had shared files. Music files, movie files…they'd e-mailed and IM'd each other regularly. And once a week he'd send her a large backup file from his laptop so that if it ever crashed, she could just send him back what he needed. She'd done the same. She'd saved all her stuff, *and* Blake's, in her Yahoo account. All she had to do was get to another computer. *"Who are you?"*

"Check the demos. That's the key."

"What?" Kenzie clutched the phone. "What does that mean? Who are—"

But she knew before she even finished her sentence

that he was gone. But who was he? A friend of Blake's? *"Dammit."*

"Shh!" everyone around her hissed.

*Yeah, yeah, fine.* But the prickle in the back of her neck hadn't gone away. She got to her feet and moved to the end of the aisle, peeking around the corner just in time to catch sight of the back of a guy running away. No red shirt this time but she knew it was the same guy she'd seen at the hospital. She hightailed it after him, but when she got to the other end of the aisle, she plowed directly into the librarian.

"No running in the library!"

"Sorry." Kenzie stepped around her, but it was too late. Her helpful mysterious caller was gone. She turned back to the librarian. "Can I use an online computer?"

"You have to sign up."

"Okay, where?"

"We're closing in half an hour, and the computers are in use until then. How about the morning?"

"Fine." She'd spend tonight going through the boat and Blake's place for anything that could help her. Then she'd borrow Aidan's computer—if he let her—or come back here to prove that Blake had been set up. Because that was the only answer she was willing to accept.

Someone had framed him, was *still* framing him.

And she was going to find out who.

AT THE STATION, Aidan was run ragged by one call after another. Near the end of the shift, his unit was called out to a secondary fire at the hardware store, where the explosion from two days ago had killed Tracy. Looking at the scene woke Aidan right up. The new fire wasn't from any smoldering spark left over from the explosion. No way. This fire had been set.

Purposely.

In a wire mesh trash can.

Tommy was already there, and at the look on Aidan's face, shook his head. "Don't start."

"Arson."

"I said don't start."

"Let me guess. We're not going to have this conversation."

"Bingo." Tommy sounded extremely tense. "And this time I'll tell you why." He got up in Aidan's face. "Because I'm close, okay? I'm very, *very* close to finishing this. So you need to let me do just that. Got it?"

Aidan didn't see that he had a choice. Later, back at the station, he stretched out on the station couch, closing his bleary eyes, needing to think.

Somehow it was all connected, he just knew it… He fell asleep trying to piece it all together, and then dreamed of a certain hot, curvy, sweet woman. A hot, curvy, sexy woman who happened to also be a *thief*.

He woke up when someone sat on him.

And then bounced on him.

Opening his eyes, he met Cristina's frowning ones. "Trying to sleep here."

"No, you're not. Your eyes are open."

"Watch this." He closed them again.

She bounced again, a maneuver that threatened to break his legs. "How's Blake's sister?"

"Why are you asking me?"

"Because you're sleeping with her. Is she okay?"

He shook his head. "How? How do you know what I barely know?"

"Rumor mill." Her derisive humor hid her misery. Cristina was hurting. Hurting over losing Blake, her partner. Hurting over somehow blowing it with Dustin. She was so hard on the outside that they all forgot how soft and sensitive she was deep inside. She'd loved Blake like a brother, and cared about Kenzie by default.

"How is she, Aidan?"

"I don't know," he answered honestly.

"What do you mean you don't know?"

"She hasn't returned my phone calls."

"So you're losing your touch, too." She broke off, momentarily distracted when Dustin walked into the room.

The tall, tough-bodied, soft-hearted EMT pushed up his glasses, glanced at Cristina and a muscle jumped in his jaw.

Cristina didn't appear to breathe. Five agonizing seconds passed, and finally, she looked away first.

Dustin merely sighed.

The two of them had been doing some kind of emotional tap dance for weeks now. Dustin said he wanted more. Cristina said she didn't.

Now the tension in the room was so thick Aidan could hardly even see them anymore. "Hey, here's an idea. You two could lust after each other in secret and then ignore each other in person. Because it's not awkward at all."

"Shut up, Aidan." Cristina sent a glare in Dustin's direction, one that said *you're an idiot.*

Without a word, Dustin walked away, into the kitchen.

Cristina expelled a low breath.

"Looks like I'm not the only one losing my touch," Aidan noted. "What did you do?"

"How do you know I did something?"

*"Please."*

Cristina sighed. "He's got his panties all unraveled because I went out with an ex."

"Ouch."

"No. No ouch. It was just dinner for God's sake. No biggee."

"Yeah. But it was dinner with a guy you've gotten naked with."

She shrugged, but dejection had settled over her pretty features. "Whatever."

"Cristina."

"I told you, it was just dinner." She got off of his legs, making sure to get an elbow in his gut. "And if he can't see that then screw him."

"Why don't you just talk to him? Tell him the truth?"

"Talking isn't what I want." She headed outside, slamming the door as she went.

Aidan's cell rang and he leaped for it, hoping for Kenzie, but he got Tommy instead.

"Might want to get down to county," the inspector said in an undecipherable tone.

"Why?"

"Because I had your girlfriend arrested."

"You arrested Kenzie?"

"You have another girlfriend I don't know about?"

"She's not my—" He pinched the bridge of his nose. "What the hell happened?"

"She's in for trespassing and interfering with a crime scene, so you figure it out. You don't control your women very well."

"She's not my woman!"

"Either way, I'd hurry. Oh, and get your checkbook. This date's going to cost you big."

# *11*

JAIL WASN'T NEARLY as adventurous as it'd been that time Kenzie had been arrested on her soap. Then she'd had a costume director and a makeup artist. Oh, and nice, soft, flattering lights. Plus she'd been able to walk off the set when the director had yelled "cut", and had sipped her iced tea and laughed it all off.

No such luxuries today.

Real life sucked.

She was given her phone call—which went to her attorney, who promised to work on getting her out. With Kenzie's own checkbook, of course.

After several hours in a holding cell, during which she contemplated the odd and unwelcome turn her life had taken, and also chewed on a few nails, she was handed her see-through baggie of personal belongings—that was twice in two days—and shown the door.

Standing in front of it wasn't her attorney, but her own gorgeous, personal savior.

Aidan was dressed in his firefighter uniform, which told her he'd come right from the job. He still wore his firefighter badass expression, too, and was looking more than a little bit temperamental as well.

*Yeah.* Not exactly thrilled to see her.

Nor was she thrilled to see him.

Okay, so a little part of her was. The bad girl part of her, which reared its horny head and begged *Oh, please can we have him just one more time?*

She ignored that and her quivery belly, and tried to brush past him.

"What, no thank you?" He shifted so that she was forced to bump into him.

Backing up, she put her hands on her hips and sent him a glare as mean as she could conjure up after a few hours spent in jail. "I didn't call you."

"Yeah. I noticed."

There were several people milling around, all from a different part of society than she was used to. The guy closest to her might have been fifty, or a hundred and fifty, it was hard to tell with the multitude of hats and coats he was wearing, despite it being summer. He pulled out a cigarette and a match, and even though she saw it coming, when he struck the match to the matchbox and the little *whoosh* hit her ears, she cringed.

Aidan was there in a second, holding her steady, which only further embarrassed her. "Easy."

"Damn." She let out a shaky breath. "What *is* that?"

"Post traumatic—"

She waggled a finger in his face. "Don't say it."

"—stress. Why didn't you call me, Kenzie?"

"Who did?"

"Tommy."

"Rat-fink bastard." It was coming back to her, her childhood here—the small town mentality, the utter lack of secrets, the way everyone stuck their nose in everyone else's business. She'd had enough of that from her early years to last her a lifetime.

She and Blake had been kept together as they'd gone into the child care protective services, where they'd landed in a total of three foster homes, each as kind and as warm as they could possibly be, and for that she was more than grateful, she was also lucky—but she'd never really settled into any of them. She didn't tend to settle, didn't tend to get comfortable; it was what had made her so certain Aidan was the one.

Look how that had blown up in her face.

When she'd gone off to Los Angeles and begun acting, she'd found heaven. Pretending to live someone else's life, already all scripted out? Perfect. She'd loved it. *Still* loved it.

But a small part of her knew that she couldn't always rely on a script. That at some point she would have to wing it. She'd eventually need a life, a *real* one, and she'd always figured that life would somehow be entwined with her brother's, maybe even right here in Santa Rey….

But now there was nothing for her here, nothing except proving Blake's innocence.

Aidan caught her arm as she stepped outside. She yanked free and he put up his hands, letting her step away from him as they walked outside. He leaned a hip against a tree, looking big and tall and attitude-ridden as he eyed her like she was a lit fuse.

His hair had been finger-combed at best. She could smell soap and man, and the potent mix of testosterone and pheromones boggled her mind. If she lived to be two hundred years old, she'd never understand her attraction to him. Back in her L.A. world, she had access to dozens of gorgeous men. Hundreds.

But while some had been nice dalliances, none of them had ever really gotten anywhere. Probably because a good number of the men she met were like her.

Pretend.

Not Aidan. He lived life with his eyes wide open, no script needed. His job demanded a lot of him, and he was tough because of it, but he hadn't ever shied away from something just because it was hard. Except for her.

"Thanks for bailing me out," she conceded.

"Need a ride to your car? Or are you going to manage that on your own, too?"

The sun was warm and bright, and she stood still in it for a moment, tilting her head up to it, inhaling deeply. Then she turned to the man who had once been her everything. Whether she liked it or not—and for the record, she didn't—he could still stop her heart, make her pulse race, and worst of all, make her hormones stand up and shimmy. "Yeah. A ride would be great, if you don't mind."

He let out a sound that told her what he thought of that, and took her to his truck.

"About that ride…" She slowed, dragging her

feet. "Everything's still booked. Maybe there's something—"

"You know where there's something." He turned on the engine and pulled out of the lot. "At my place."

"Yeah." She shook her head. "No."

"Yeah no?"

She sighed. "It's just that staying with you seems like a whole lot of trouble I don't want to face."

"Why?"

"Because I don't want to lead you on."

"I thought you enjoyed exacting your revenge on my body."

With more than a slight twinge of regret and, *dammit,* guilt, she avoided his gaze.

"Come on, Kenz, be honest. You're not afraid of hurting me. You're afraid *you'll* get hurt."

Wasn't that the plain ugly truth.

"You made sure I understood that you'd changed," he said softly, looking over at her for a beat before returning his attention to the road. "Now you have to understand something. I've changed as well."

Yes. Yes, he had.

"Look, you wanted to know what happened all those years ago?" he asked. "I got scared, that's what the hell happened. I'd always lived my life without letting people inside my heart, where they could hurt me. But you got in, and, yeah, that terrified me. You're doing it again, by the way, getting in, and I'm not any more thrilled about it now than I was then."

Something warm slid through her at his words, and

the low, rough tone in which they were spoken. Warm, and dangerously seductive.

He pulled into his driveway and shut off the engine, turning in his seat to face her. "You'll have to make do without the five-star rating." He paused a beat. "Although there are certain five-star services I *do* offer."

When she met his gaze she saw the sparkle of pure wicked trouble in his eyes. *Oh, boy.* "Aidan—"

"I'm talking about my breakfasts, which you happened to miss out on. And then there's my massage specialty." He didn't add any obvious eyebrow waggle or other suggestive gesture, but his eyes crinkled and she knew he was *thinking* suggestively.

*Yup.* Dangerously seductive. She already knew how erotic his touch could be, just how earthy, how naughty, and she wasn't ready to go back there. Not if she intended to be the one to walk away this time.

And there would be walking away when this was over…

Even while she was thinking it, he took her hand and led her to his door. Her instinct was to make a smartass comment to piss him off, chase him away, and yet she didn't do anything but allow him to open the door for her. Once she started to step inside, he stopped her. When she met his gaze, he asked, "You planning anything else I should know about?"

"Like?"

"Shit. Anything. It could be anything."

The sun was bright. The surf behind them loud and choppy. She loved the scent of the ocean. She'd missed that, working long, long days on set in the middle of Los Angeles. Now that she'd been cancelled, she could see taking a laptop out on the beach and just writing to her heart's content if she wanted. "My immediate plans involve a shower."

"That's all?" he asked so warily that she smiled.

"Yeah. That's all."

He touched the corner of her smiling mouth. "That's a good look for you."

"What are you talking about, I smile all the time."

"On TV, maybe. But I haven't seen much of it here."

"Well, maybe that's because I was in a fire, then facing the fact that my brother's dead, and then…" And then she'd been in his bed, naked, panting, sobbing his name, holding onto his head as his mouth and then his body had taken her to heaven—

"*That* look," he said, pointing at her. "I want to know what you were thinking just then to put *that* look on your face."

She crossed her arms over her suddenly aching breasts. "Nothing."

"You are such a liar," he chided softly.

He gestured her inside his place, and she took a better look around than she had when she'd been fresh out of the hospital, and then fresh out of his bed. She saw the pretty windows, the wood floors he'd done himself, and felt another ache, this one in her chest.

She knew that growing up, Aidan hadn't had much of a stable home life, either. He'd been shuffled around as much as she had. Going into the fire academy had changed his life, given him a team, but more than that, his first *real* friendships. The kind of friendships that would last, the kind of friend that had his back no matter what. He still hadn't had any real understanding of what that meant when she'd gone off to Los Angeles, but she could tell it had come to him in the years since. There was an easy confidence about him, an air that said he'd been well liked, well taken care of...

Well loved.

Her heart did a little flop at that because she hadn't given herself the same. Oh, sure, she was liked. She'd been taken care of. But loved by someone other than Blake?

No.

And if she took away the fame, leaving just small-town girl Kenzie Stafford, what would actually be left?

The answer was as unsettling as the thought, especially given that now she really was without that fancy job. "Aidan?"

He'd headed for the kitchen, but stopped and turned to her. "Yeah?"

"Thanks."

"For?"

"For bailing me out. For waiting to make sure I was okay."

He leaned back against the wall and studied her. "So why did you do it, Kenz? Why did you go back after I'd warned you not to—" He broke off and shook his head. "Never mind. I just heard my own words and realized *exactly* why you did it. *Because* I warned you not to."

"Am I that stubborn?"

"Hell, yeah, you're that stubborn."

She rolled her eyes, then caught the flash of humor in his. He was laughing at her, and not with her, which should have made her defensive and possibly bitchy, but in spite of herself, she let out a laugh, too. "Okay, so it wasn't the smartest thing I've done. But it was the right thing."

"How about stealing my file, was that the right thing, too?"

She let out a low breath. "I was wondering when we were going to get to that."

He just looked at her, big and bad and...patient. So damn patient. She pulled the file from her bag and handed it over. "Thanks."

"I'd say you're welcome, if I'd given it to you."

"You'd have done the same thing in my position."

"You think so?"

She looked into his compelling eyes and felt her breath catch. "Okay, no. You would have asked. But maybe you're a better person than I am."

His eyes expressed his surprise at that statement. They both knew she hadn't always considered him such a great guy. "People change," she whispered, mirroring his words back to her. "Right?"

"That's right." The smile hit his eyes before his lips slowly curved, and there was an answering quiver that began in her belly. *Oh, boy.* Not good. He was standing too close, and not being annoying or antagonistic, and suddenly it all seemed too intimate.

She started to turn away but that was cowardice, and if she was going to learn anything while being back here in Santa Rey, it was not going to be that, so she faced him again. "I really am sorry for dragging you into this. For getting arrested and you having to bail me out. For driving you crazy. Pick any of the above."

"You didn't drag me into anything."

"Maybe not, but I'm about to." She let out a breath. "I need to tell you something."

"Okay." When she didn't go on, he raised an eyebrow. "Is it something that's going to get you arrested again?"

"No. I'm kind of hoping to avoid repeating that experience."

"Good."

"But there are things you should know. Things you're not going to like."

"Try me."

"Okay. I've been getting calls from someone I think is trying to help me."

He stared at her. "Your local cell caller?"

"Yes. He told me the key, whatever that means, is in Blake's computer files."

"He?"

"I think so. But I can't place the voice, he's disguised it."

"How the hell does he know the key's in Blake's computer files?" Aidan asked her.

"I don't know."

"Blake's laptop was never found. I'm betting it went up in *Blake's Girl*."

"As did mine. But with a computer, I could access my backup files, which would include Blake's backup files."

"I have a computer." He was close enough that she could see the green swirling in his light brown eyes. The scar bisecting his left eyebrow, the lines on his face, only added character, and a sexiness she couldn't have explained to save her life.

His mouth was slightly curved and she knew if she leaned in and touched hers to it, his lips would be warm and skilled, and most of all, giving.

"I didn't think I'd be happy to see you," she murmured, stepping closer. "But I've been proven wrong on two accounts now. When you saved me from the fire, and when I came out of jail and saw you standing there."

"Just the two?"

"Well, *maybe* one other time…"

Leaning close, he let his mouth brush her ear. "Try a couple."

At the reminder of how he'd made her come *several* times, easily she might add, as if he knew her body better than she did, a little shiver of awareness went down her spine, chased by another one, this one pure anticipation.

He could do it again. He could take her there again, to heaven, to oblivion… Only this time it wouldn't be adrenaline. This time she'd go in with her eyes wide open. His needed to be as well.

"I was worried about you," he murmured. "You've got to stay out of this one, Kenzie. Stay out of Tommy's way."

Somehow her face was nuzzling his throat, and she was trying to breathe him in. "I'm going to prove Blake's innocence in all this," she told him, liking the feel of her lips against his skin. "No matter the cost."

"Even if the price is my friendship?"

Her throat actually tightened at the thought and she pulled back to look into his eyes. "Is it going to cost me that?"

"Depends." He took her hand, put it on his chest and offered her a smile. "You still intending on stomping all over my tender heart?"

At that, and the crinkles at the corners of his eyes, the ones telling her he was teasing her, she out and out laughed, feeling much of tension drain away. "Yes."

His hands went to her hips, pulling her closer, and she stared into his face, feeling so at home in his house that she found herself hesitating, not for the first time that day, and wishing she had a script for what came next.

"You're thinking again," he murmured.

"Yeah."

He leaned back against the front door, unexpectedly giving her space. Space she thought she'd wanted, but found she didn't want at all. "I really did intend to stomp all over your heart, you know. When I first saw you again, I wanted to hurt you the way you'd hurt me. But then we kissed."

"We did a lot more than kiss."

She flashed back to that night, when she'd climbed into bed with him, pressing her icy feet to his, then her body. She remembered realizing he was naked and warm and strong and hard…*God*. He'd been so utterly irresistible, she'd lost her head. And, yeah, they'd done a lot more than kiss. "Fine. We kissed, and then I decided I should sleep with you and then walk away. Perfect, neat revenge."

"Neat, maybe. But not perfect." His eyes were glittering with knowledge, hard won. "Because it wasn't as easy as you thought, was it?"

No, it hadn't been. Because it'd been amazing between them. So damned amazing. "Maybe I've been looking at this wrong."

He didn't move from the door, just kept looking at her, his eyes warm, his mouth curved, his body big and bad and so gorgeous she could hardly stand it.

She wanted him.

Again.

Still.

"Maybe it's not about sleeping with you once and walking away," she heard herself say. "Maybe it's about letting this thing take its own lead for as long as I'm here."

"'This thing'? You mean the way we apparently can't stay out of each other's pants?"

At the huskiness in his voice, her nipples hardened. "Yes."

# *12*

AIDAN PUSHED AWAY from the door and came toward Kenzie, all easy, loose-limbed confidence, yet radiating an intensity that made her breath catch. He didn't stop until they were toe-to-toe, and she slowly tipped up her head to look into his inscrutable eyes.

"You want to have sex," he said silkily. "Here. Tonight. Now."

Her breath caught at his bluntness. "And then maybe again later."

"Later," he repeated, as if trying to process this.

"Maybe even until I leave Santa Rey. At which time we both walk away, eyes wide open."

He just stared at her for the longest moment. "What happened to trouncing on my heart?"

"It seems you were right. I don't really want to hurt you."

When he shot her a not-buying-it look, she caved. "Okay, so I want to hurt you less than I want to sleep with you again."

"You know, you'd think I'd be tough enough to walk away from such an overwhelmingly romantic offer," he said drily, sounding both intrigued and baffled. "But apparently…" He put his hands on her hips. "I'm not."

She offered a smile that was sheer nerve. "So…yes?"

His eyes never wavered, holding hers, leveling her as he pulled her in. "I don't know, Kenzie. I'm a little afraid…"

"Be serious."

His smile was crooked and impossibly endearing. "I am. This time you could really do it, whether you're trying to or not. This time, you just might take out my heart."

"Come on," she quipped, even as a part of her was afraid he was right, for both of them. "If we're just having a physical relationship and nothing else, how can we get hurt?"

With a soft laugh, he slid his hands up her spine, and then back again, low enough now to cup her butt and squeeze.

He was hard.

Bending his head, he put his mouth to her ear and let out a breath that made her shiver in longing. "Just a physical relationship, Kenzie? Is that all this is? Really?" He sank his teeth into her lobe and she shivered again.

"It—it's all it *should* be," she managed.

Another soft, deprecating laugh rumbled through his chest, this one aimed at the both of them. "Okay, well as long as we're being honest, you should know…" His hands glided up her spine again, this time beneath her shirt to touch bare skin. "Even though you *are* going to hurt me, it's not enough to make me say no. Truth is, nothing could…"

She opened her mouth to say something, but then he kissed the spot he'd just nipped at, soothing the ache as his fingers stroked over her skin. Her eyes drifted shut, and she slid her arms around his neck, pressing close. "No pain, no gain," she whispered, and he let out another low laugh as he lifted her up and carried her to his bedroom.

To his bed.

He settled over her, looking down into her face for a beat before lowering his head and taking her mouth with his demanding one.

If simply walking into his house had felt like a homecoming, then this, here, now, felt even more so. He felt like home, he smelled like home, and he tasted even better; she hesitated, thinking, *uh-oh*.

His hands came up to hold her face. "What?"

She stared up into his eyes and saw herself reflected there, as if they were one, and although it was deeply unsettling to realize that this time she could fall even harder for him—if she let herself—she also couldn't imagine walking away, without being in his arms again.

"Kenz?"

"Nothing, it's nothing." And she pulled him down for another kiss as the heat of him seeped into her bones, warming her with a sensual promise of what was to come. Those big, warm hands slid along her arms, lifting them up over her head, entwining their fingers as his mouth continued to plunder hers, delivering on that promise.

It was familiar, and it was comforting, and yet it was so, so much more as well. Not since being with Aidan six years ago had she given any thought to what it would be like to be with a guy long enough that he felt…like home. She was a woman who liked change, who liked the new and exciting, who lived off the lines someone else wrote for her each day.

But with Aidan, she knew what he felt like, what he tasted like, exactly how crazy he could drive her with a touch of a single finger, and yet being with him felt almost unbearably *right,* and far more arousing than she could have ever imagined.

Still kissing her, he pulled off her top, then her skirt. Her new bra was a front hook, which didn't slow him down at all, and when he had her naked except her panties, he hooked his fingers in the thin strip of cotton on her hips and let his gaze meet hers. Then he tugged, slipping the underwear down her legs and off, sailing them over one shoulder. Towering over her, fully dressed while she was as naked as she could get, he let out a low breath. "You're so beautiful."

"And you're overdressed." Still in his fire gear, in fact…

"In a minute." He was kneeling between her legs. He spread his, which in turn spread hers, and his gaze took her in, in one fell swoop, heating her skin everywhere he looked. He traced his fingers over her breasts, her belly, her thighs.

Between.

When he bent his head with fierce intent, she sucked in a breath, a breath that clogged her throat when he replaced his fingers with his mouth.

"Aidan," she managed, hardly recognizing her own voice. "I—"

His tongue encircled her tender, sensitized flesh, making her quiver from the inside out, and she promptly forgot what she'd meant to say. While his tongue and fingers circled and teased and stroked, she gripped the sheets and stared down at him. His hair stood up, from her fingers, she realized. His eyes were closed, his expression dreamy as he brought her such bliss she could hardly even see, much less think.

But she didn't close her eyes. She watched him concentrate on her pleasure as if it were his own, took in his moves, the moves that were driving her right out of her ever-loving mind.

It was as if he knew what made her tick, inside and out. That was a terrifying thought, really. Because the girl he'd once known no longer existed, and since then…well, she hadn't really let anyone know her.

An ever-changing script.

That was her life.

A life she was no longer sure about. But having him take her apart the way he was, *that* she was sure about.

He opened his eyes, so molten hot that they were nearly black, and looked up at her. He was sure, too, which should have stopped her cold, and she stirred. "Aidan—"

"Shh."

Then he swirled his tongue in a precise rhythm over ground zero, and she lost it.

Completely.

Lost.

It.

Panting for breath, arching up off the mattress and into his mouth, she dug her fingers into the sheets, throwing her head back at the peak, sobbing out his name.

Slowly he brought her back to planet earth. She closed her eyes, savoring the pleasure, still quivering and pulsing as he kissed his way back up her body, his tongue stroking a rib, a nipple, her throat…and then he cupped her face and smiled at her.

"You shushed me," she said, her voice sounding weak and raspy.

"It was for a good cause." He rocked his hips into hers.

"I'm going to get you back for that."

He smiled wickedly. "Should I be scared?"

"Terrified." Rolling him over, she sat on him and tugged his uniform shirt off. She could have spent a year lapping him up with nothing but her tongue. He had a tight body, toned from years of physical labor. His chest was broad, hard, his belly rippled with sinew and rising and falling in a way that assured her she was in no way alone in this almost chemical-like attraction they shared, which transcended both time and logic.

His hands went to the button on his pants to help speed up the process, and she ran her fingers up the taut, corded muscles of his abs. He unzipped, she tugged, and then nearly drooled at the sight of the part of him so happy to see her.

She licked her lips.

He groaned.

She kissed him, on the very tip.

"Kenz—" he choked out, tunneling his fingers through her hair.

Since her mouth was now full, she couldn't answer, and he said something completely unintelligible anyway, which, she had to admit, only egged her on. God, she loved rendering this big, bad, tough man completely incapable of speech. Loved the power that surged through her at the way he was breathing, saying her name.

Loved so much about it that it scared her. Scared her into being even more bold and brazen so that she didn't have to think about how much being with him meant to her.

How much he meant to her.

Using her hands and mouth, she drew him to the edge. "Two-minute warning," he groaned out, his hands fisted in the sheets at his sides as she ran her tongue up his length. "Okay, thirty seconds. *Maybe*."

She kept going until he swore and grabbed a condom, nudging her to her back, his hands running up the undersides of her arms until they were over her head. His knee spread her legs, his thigh rubbing against the core of her.

"In," she gasped, arching into him. "In me now."

Lowering his body to hers, he nipped at her lower lip, then kissed her, hard and deep, his tongue slipping into her mouth at the very moment he slipped into her body. "Like that?"

She couldn't answer. Hell, she could hardly breathe.

"Kenzie?"

"Yes," she managed, then shuddered as he withdrew, only to thrust into her again. And again. *"Like that."*

The feel of him, thick and hot and filling her to the brink, had her gasping his name, wrapping her legs around his hips, leaving her unable to remember exactly what she was supposedly paying him back for. Her toes were curling, her skin feeling too tight for her body, which seemed to swell from the inside out. "Aidan—"

"Come," he demanded, grinding his teeth in what looked like agony. "I want to feel you come before I—"

She burst in mindless, blind sensation, and barely heard his strangled answering groan as he exploded.

For long moments afterward, they lay there entwined, panting and damp, and powerless to move, their breathing echoing loudly through the bedroom.

"Is it just me," she finally managed, "or does that get better and better?"

"Oh, yeah."

She fell quiet a moment, but then couldn't resist. "You think it'll keep happening? You know, until I leave?"

"If it does, it's likely to kill me."

"Yes." She sighed dreamily. "But what a way to go."

His soft huff of laughter was the last thing she remembered before she drifted off to sleep.

AIDAN WOKE UP SOMETIME LATER with a smile, his body ready for another round. In the pitch-dark, he rolled over for Kenzie.

And got nothing.

With a very bad feeling in his gut, he sat up. "You're gone, aren't you?" he said into the night.

When he got no answer, he tossed back the covers and got out of bed, but it was too late. She had left. He told himself he wasn't her keeper, and she could go wherever she wanted, but he'd been lulled into the impression that she hadn't been done with him yet.

She *wasn't* done with him, not yet. Which meant she was probably out there looking to poke her nose into the arsons. Aidan hurriedly got dressed. He had no idea where she was but he needed to find out, because with whatever information she'd get, she'd go snooping into things that were guaranteed to piss off Tommy.

*Hell.* They'd just spent hours in his bed. And in his shower. And then his bed again. Hadn't he tired her out?

His stomach was grumbling and his head starting to pound when he picked up his cell phone and called hers; he was shocked when she answered.

"Hi," she said in that soft, breathless voice that had only a few hours before made him come.

Just hearing it stirred him halfway to life. He was little better than Pavlov's dogs. "Where are you?"

"Oh, out and about." She still sounded breathless.

"Kenzie, what are you doing?"

"Um…exercising?"

"That's a bad word to you."

"Not anymore. Do you have any idea how much work it takes to stay in TV shape?"

And then he heard it, the unmistakable sound of a sliding door either opening or closing. "Where are you?"

"Whoops, bad connection," she said.

He gnashed his teeth together. "We have a great connection. What are you up to?"

"Wow, I can hardly hear you…"

"Kenz—"

"Gotta go."

He didn't have to hear the click to know she'd shut her phone. Nor did he bother with swearing. Instead, he grabbed his keys and went after her, figuring her options were severely limited. She wouldn't have gone back to the docks because there were no sliding door there. So she was probably at Blake's house. He supposed she could also be at any one of the arsons Blake had been accused of, but most of them had been demo'd, and plus it seemed likely that if she was butting her nose in, she'd start at the top.

So would he.

He hit the jackpot on his first try. Pulling into the small house Blake had claimed as his own, he parked right next to Kenzie's flashy Mercedes. He got out of his truck and felt the hood of her car.

Still warm.

So she hadn't been there long. She was just damn lucky she hadn't gotten herself arrested again, considering the yellow tape surrounding the house. Just thinking about what Tommy would say, and how long he'd jail her this time, had him sweating. The front door was shut and, as he discovered, locked.

Aidan moved around the side of the house. His plan was simple. He was going to scare the hell out of her. And then he was going to kiss the hell out of her.

And then…and then he had no idea. Spanking her seemed like a good option.

The sliding back door on Blake's deck was unlocked and opened an inch. This was where she'd entered, and following suit, he slipped inside. The place was dark, but there was a light on upstairs, and he headed in that direction. At a sound behind him, he whipped around just as two hands smacked him in the chest and shoved. As he fell back, he reached out and hauled his assailant with him. He hit his ass on the bottom step and Kenzie landed on him.

*"What are you doing?"* she demanded.

The stairs biting into his back, her full weight over the top of him, he hissed out a breath of pain. "What am *I* doing? What are *you* doing?"

"I'm—" She bit back whatever she'd been about to say, crawled backward off of him and stood up.

"No, it's okay, I'm fine, thanks," he muttered, getting up on his own and brushing himself off. "How did you get in here?"

"Blake gave me his spare key a long time ago."

"Okay, so back to my first question. Why are you here?"

"Looking for clues to Blake's innocence." She glared at him, then pointed to the door. "You need to leave."

"So do you."

"Oh, no. This is my brother's place. I'm his beneficiary. I get to be here."

"Not with the caution tape still blocking the front door, you don't."

She was breathing fast, her voice thick and husky as if she'd been crying. Or maybe she still was. He couldn't see her clearly enough to decide. "Ah, Kenzie. Don't—"

"Go," she said, crossing her arms over her chest.

"Fine. But you're coming with me."

"No, I'm not."

"Yeah, you are." Wrapping his fingers around her arm, he headed toward the sliding door, toting her with him, until she yanked free. Then, lifting her nose, she stalked out in front of him, going willingly but not happily. "Kenzie," he said as she got into her car.

"I don't want to talk right now." She tried to shut the driver's door on him but he stepped closer, holding it open.

"Isn't that convenient."

"Dammit, Aidan. Get out of my way."

"Just tell me where you're going."

For the first time, she hesitated.

"You could try my house," he suggested. "My computer."

She paused another beat. "I wouldn't want to impose."

"Imposing would be getting your pretty ass arrested again, goddammit. Meet me there."

"Fine." Putting the car into gear, she peeled out, leaving him little choice but to hope that she would.

# *13*

WITH LITTLE TO NO TRAFFIC in the middle of the night, it took only five minutes to get home. Aidan pulled into his driveway next to the little red sports car, watching Kenzie storm up the walk to his front door, looking irritated and frustrated.

Just as irritated and frustrated, he followed. Did she have no clue what she was doing to him?

How could she not?

"Wait," she said, stopping so fast he plowed into her, staring back at the street. "Did you see that car?"

"No."

"It was gray." She chewed on her thumbnail. "Look, I'm not trying to change the subject here, because trust me, I'm pissed and enjoying being pissed, but I think someone's following me."

Reaching past her, he unlocked the door and gestured her in ahead of him, keeping his body in front of her back as he turned to eye the street.

He didn't see the car—at the moment, there were *no* cars—but he didn't doubt her. "You've seen it before?"

"Yes. Truthfully, I'm beginning to feel sort of

stalked." She whirled to face him. "Okay, so back to being pissed off."

Oh, no. Not yet. He'd anticipated her, and was standing so close she bumped into him, squeaking in surprise, but when she tried to take a step back, he held her still. Christ, she smelled good and the way her hair framed her face… "How long have you suspected someone's been following you?"

"Since the boat fire, I guess."

"Have you told anyone? Tommy? The police?"

"I wasn't really sure. I'm still not sure. It's just a feeling."

He let go of her to pull out his cell phone.

"What are you doing?"

"Calling the police."

Kenzie stepped close and shut the phone, stuffing it back into his pocket. "Aidan, listen to me. We both know that you and I don't do *real* relationships, especially not with each other. Now sex, we do that just fine. And in case you're confused, the biggest difference between the two is that with just sex, there's no sharing of personal information."

He was not liking where this was going. At all. "Meaning?"

"Meaning I don't have to account to you, and you're not responsible for me."

He stared at her, more stung than he'd like to admit. "Well, shit."

"I mean it, Aidan."

"You don't want me to call the police."

"And scare off the guy? No, I don't."

"Fine."

"*Fine*. Now where the hell is your computer? We have some files to access."

"My bedroom."

They were nose-to-nose, now. Breathing in each other's air. He could feel the heat of her radiating into him, and for whatever reason, his hands ran down her arms and then back up again, squeezing a little, more moved by the close proximity than he'd like to admit.

The very tips of her breasts brushed against his shirt. Her thighs bumped into his. Sparks were flying from her eyes, her mouth grim.

A mouth that suddenly he couldn't stop looking at.

Her hands had come up to his chest and she dug her fingers into his pecs, hard enough to have him hissing out a breath. Her eyes were on his, but then they lowered to his mouth.

She was thinking about kissing him.

Leaning in, he took care of that little piece of business for her. Covering her mouth with his, he swallowed her little moan of pleasure and promptly lost himself in her when she melted against him, entwining her arms around his neck so tightly he couldn't breathe. Since breathing was overrated anyway, especially when kissing her, he just hauled her up tighter against him and kept at it. Her hands were in his hair, his molded the length of her body to him, until suddenly, she shoved him clear, turned and stalked off, heading down the hallway and into his bedroom. He stared after her, breathing like a misused race horse, warring with himself. He could go after her. Or *he* could walk out on *her* for a change of pace.

*Yeah, right.* He went after her.

WHEN AIDAN OPENED THE DOOR of his bedroom, Kenzie held her breath. She hadn't turned on the light, so he was silhouetted from behind by the lamp in the living room, looking tall, dark, and so sexy she could hardly stand it.

And attitude-ridden. Don't forget that. Stalking past her, he opened his laptop and hit the power button. While it booted up, she just stared through the dim room at him, wishing…hell.

Wishing things were different. That's all. If only she could call the writers and complain about this particular plotline, and maybe get it adjusted. Or get a new script delivered. Yeah, that would be best. One with a happy ending, please. With a sigh, she moved to the laptop. "Should I download it to your desktop?"

"Yes."

She accessed her mail, and the files she'd saved, clicking on the first of Blake's. "It's going to take a while. It's a big file. And it'll take even longer to flip through it all and see if there's even anything in it that we can use."

"Your caller suggested there was."

"Yes, but how did he know? *What* did he know?"

"Let's find out. Kenzie—"

"I'm not ready to talk."

He stepped closer, a big, tall, badass outline. "What *are* you ready for?"

"How about the only thing we're good at?"

With a low sound that might have been an agreeing groan, he came even closer. "Kenzie—"

"No. I mean it." He was hard. She could feel him. Could feel, too, the tension shimmering throughout his entire body. It matched hers. "No talking."

"Fine." With a rough tug, he hauled her up against him. His body was warm and corded with strength, his hands hard and hot on her. And his mouth…

God, his mouth.

He was the most amazing kisser, his lips warm and soft and firm all at the same time, his tongue both talented and greedy and generous.

So generous that she moaned into his mouth and held on for the ride until she couldn't stand it anymore. "Clothes," she muttered, and yanked off her own top, gratified to see him doing the same. She stared through the dark at his bared torso as she worked the buttons on her jeans while simultaneously kicking off her shoes. God, he was gorgeous. Sleek, toned and so damned yummy she wanted to gobble him up on the spot. She shoved down her jeans, watching him do the same, but unlike her, his underwear went bye-bye with his jeans, and her mouth actually went dry.

Riveted by the sight, she stood there in her bra and panties and socks. Staring.

He stood there in nothing. In glorious, mouth-dropping, heart-stopping nothing. Yeah, she'd seen it before, all of it and more—*but, damn.*

"You cheated," he said, reaching for her bra.

His erection nudged her belly, and forgetting to finish stripping, she wrapped her fingers around him.

He hissed out a breath.

"Too tight?" she asked as she stroked.

"No, your fingers are frozen."

For some reason that made her laugh. How the hell that was even possible with all the sensations crowding and pushing for space in her brain was beyond her but she stood there, her fingers wrapped around a very impressive erection and laughed.

"Yeah, see, you're not really supposed to hold onto a guy's favorite body part and laugh."

Which, of course, made her laugh harder.

With a shake of his head, he just smiled, clearly not too worried because he remained hard as a rock in her hand...

As his fingers worked their magic and her bra fell to the floor at their feet.

When he stepped even closer, her nipples brushed his chest, and it was her turn to hiss in a breath as they hardened.

And then she couldn't breathe at all because he dropped to his knees, hooked his thumbs in the edge of her panties and tugged.

At the sight he revealed, he gave a low, ragged groan and slid his hands up the backs of her thighs, cupping her bottom in his big palms. "God, look at you."

"Aidan—"

"You're so pretty here." He ran a finger over her. "All wet and glistening. For me." There was a deep, husky satisfaction to his voice that made her thighs quiver.

"Spread your legs," he murmured, skimming hot, wet, openmouthed kisses up an inner thigh. "Yeah, like that." He pulled her forward, and right into his mouth.

At the first unerring stroke of his tongue her knees nearly buckled but he had a grip on her, one hand on her hip, holding her upright, the other exploring between her legs, working with his tongue to drive her out of her mind. "Aidan—"

"You taste like heaven," he whispered against her. *"Heaven."*

And he felt like it. She strained against him, her fingers tunneled into his hair, her head thrown back as he took her exactly where he wanted to her to go, which was to the very edge of a cliff, so high she couldn't see all the way to the bottom, couldn't speak, couldn't do anything but feel.

And she was feeling plenty. Mostly a need for speed at this point, but he purposely slowed her down, dancing his tongue over her as light as a feather. She tightened her fingers in his hair, silently threatening to make him bald if he didn't get back to business. Her business. "Aidan, dammit."

"I could look at you all day."

"Look later. Do now."

"Always in a hurry." He tsked, but obliged.

Oh, God, how he obliged, skimming his hands up

the front of her thighs, gently opening her. For a moment he pulled back, admiring the sight before him, wet from his tongue, wet from her own arousal.

Standing there so open and vulnerable, she let out a growl of frustration and need, and he leaned in, this time sucking her into his mouth hard, giving her the rhythm she needed to completely lose it.

When her knees gave out, he let her fall, catching her, rising to his feet, spinning toward the bed, his mouth fastened to hers. His hands moved over her body, thoroughly, ruthlessly, ravenously kissing her as they went, until from somewhere behind them, from the pocket of her pants, her cell phone went off. She couldn't even think about getting it. Hell, the entire place could have gone up in flames right then and there and she doubted she would have thought about it. "In me, in me."

He let out a rough laugh.

*"Now."*

Because now was the only thing that mattered, and this was the only thing that registered, the feel of his hands on her body, molding, sculpting, flaming the wildfire flickering to life inside her.

Aidan crawled up her body. He'd found a condom, and made himself at home between her thighs. Then he stared down into her eyes, his unwavering and fierce. "This is not just sex." His voice was low and rough. "It's not. Not for me."

She blinked, trying to clear her fuzzy head.

"And if that's all it is for you, I want to know it now."

He lifted her hips, his strong callused fingers gliding over her flesh, making sure she was ready for him.

She was.

Beyond ready.

"Tell me," he demanded, holding still, waiting on her word. She stared up at him, her heart swelling at the truth. "It's more," she admitted, which—*ding, ding, ding*—was the right answer because then he spread her thighs wider and drove himself into her, hard and fast, the way she'd wanted, and took her right where she needed to go.

Halfway there, with her breath sobbing in her throat, with their bodies straining with each other, she cupped his jaw and looked into his face.

He was damp with sweat, hard with tension, and so damned sexy she could scarcely speak. "Aidan."

"Don't stop me."

She shook her head at his rough plea. Stop him? Was he kidding? She wanted him to never stop.

Never…a terrifying thought. "Aidan…"

His mouth nuzzled at her ear. "Yeah?"

"I missed you," she whispered, letting him in on her biggest secret, giving it to him without reserve, letting him look deeply into her eyes.

She absorbed both his surprise and his next thrust, and then that was it.

She burst.

And so did he.

# 14

AIDAN LAY ON HIS BACK, a hot, naked, still quivering Kenzie in his arms, and let her words soak in.

*She'd missed him.* "Kenz?"

"Mmm." Her face was pressed against his throat, her mouth sending shivers of delight down his spine even now, when his bones had turned into overcooked noodles and he couldn't have moved to save his life.

Well, except a certain part of his anatomy, which appeared to have segregated from his brain. That part moved. That part wanted round two.

And possibly round three, please.

Kenzie lifted her head and looked at him, all sleepy-eyed and still glowing. Waiting for him to speak.

He found himself cupping her face, and bringing it in for a kiss that lingered.

And deepened.

"I missed you, too," he whispered against her lips.

She pulled back and closed her eyes.

Staring down at her, he let out a breath. Okay. So she hadn't meant it. It'd just been the heat of the moment talking. He supposed he could understand that. Had to understand that. After all, the moment had gotten pretty damn heated. "It's all right." God, listen to him lie. "I get it."

Across the room sat his laptop, with answers. Or so he hoped. "We'd better get up." He was relieved to note that his voice seemed to sound normal, that he was still breathing and that the heart she'd just stabbed was apparently still in working order.

Even if it was bleeding all over the place. Internal carnage...

But he had no one to blame but himself for opening it up to her in the first place. She'd warned him, hadn't she? She'd warned him and he'd been cocky enough not to believe it possible.

"Aidan?"

He managed to look at her.

"I *did* miss you. I missed this. But..."

"But life intrudes. I get that, too."

She looked into his eyes, sighed, then slipped from the bed. Gloriously naked, she walked to his computer. Lit only by the glow of the screen, she afforded him a particularly fine view. "Huh," she said, and bent over a little so that her fingers could move over the keyboard.

She was absolutely clueless about the picture she made in green glowing profile, with her hair wild around her head, a whisker burn from his face across a breast and her ribs, and her very sweet ass looking good enough to bite.

"That's odd," she muttered, her fingers moving

faster, the furrow between her eyebrows deepening as she frowned.

He opened his mouth to ask what was odd, but she bent a little farther and he couldn't gather enough working brain cells to do anything but stare. Her spine was narrow and pretty, and his gaze followed it down past the indention of her waist and the gentle flare of her hips to one of his favorite parts of a woman's anatomy. Her legs were spread slightly, her thighs taut, allowing him a peek of the treasure between—

"Aidan?"

At the tone, he managed to squelch the lust. *Barely.* Rising, he walked up behind her. Also naked. Curling his body around hers from behind, a good amount of that lust came barreling back, hitting him like a freight train. He couldn't help it. His chest was against her back, her world-class ass pressed into his crotch. His hands went to her hips, one slipping around to her ribs, his fingers just brushing the underside of her breast. Pressing his lips to the side of her neck, he let his hand skim up, gliding over her nipple, which hardened gratifyingly in his fingers.

*Oh, yeah.*

His other hand slid to her belly and began a southward descent—

"Look." Catching his hand, she pointed to an opened Excel worksheet. She had brought up an interesting list. "My mysterious caller said to look at the demos," she told him. "I didn't know what he meant, but all the burned buildings have been razed to the ground. I saw the photos in Zach's file—not all of those buildings were severely damaged."

With great difficulty, he frowned at the computer and not at her nude body, his hands still full with warm, sweet, sexy-as-hell woman. "It's true," he said. "But the properties were demolished anyway. Except for the last two."

"On whose orders?"

"The records have been sealed."

"Why?"

"That's the question. Zach tried to get the answer to that and it cost him."

Forcing his concentration from her body, he took in the worksheet in front of him. "Pretty impressive information here." Blake had been busy.

So had he been keeping track of his own handi-work, along with what happened to each property after the fires?

"Who has the power to order a demolition of a burned property?" Kenzie asked him.

"The owner, anyone acting on the behalf of an owner or the fire department, if the property is deemed unstable or unsafe for any reason."

She pulled free and went for her clothes, which were strewn across the room. He watched with great regret as she found the pieces one by one and covered up that gorgeous bod.

With a sigh, he reached for his jeans and slid them on. Back to the grown-up world apparently… "How is it you've never looked through Blake's files before?"

"I never thought to. We regularly sent each other files, just in case. It was our backup system."

"What did you send him?"

She lifted a shoulder. "Rough drafts of stuff."

"Stuff?"

"I've been writing. Scripts." Another lift of her shoulder. "For the day I finally ate too many donuts and didn't get asked to audition anymore."

"I bet you're a great writer."

"Really?"

He thought about how deeply she felt things, how good she was with words, and nodded.

Looking touched, she smiled. "Thanks."

"How long ago did he send you this file?"

"He sent me a backup file every week. We were supposed to keep only the latest version for each other, but I was always too lazy to go back and delete the week before, so I should have them all—" She stared at him for a beat before whipping back to the computer. Her fingers raced over the keys as he bent his head close to hers, looking at what she brought up.

An entire list of arson-related backup files from Blake, starting shortly after the first suspicious fires, until the day before he died.

"So," she said slowly. "Either he was a damned stupid felon, or he was investigating the arsons himself."

Her tone made it clear which she believed.

"Or," he said softly, knowing she was going to hate him. "He's keeping track of the arsons for a partner."

She looked at him again, her eyes cooling to, oh, about thirty-five degrees below zero.

"Open the first file."

Without a word, she clicked on it. It was a Word document, a diary of notes with a running commentary. The first read:

*Hill Street fire:*
*Second point of origin mysteriously vanished on day of cleanup. Wire metal trash can, unique enough in design that it should be traceable. When I mentioned this to the chief, he said I should stick to fighting fires.*

Kenzie read the entry out loud, twice, then scrolled down to the next entry, several weeks later.

*Blood is thicker than water. I was told that today and apparently need to remember it. If I want to live.*

Kenzie whipped her gaze to Aidan. "What the hell does that mean?"

"Sounds like a threat," he said grimly.

"Blood is thicker than water," she repeated. "Who is he talking about? We have no family. At least no family who cares about us, anyway."

He hated the look on her face, the faraway, distant, self-protective look she got whenever she had to talk about her past. There was no doubt, she and Blake had had it rough growing up, being shuffled from one foster home to another. The saving grace was that they'd been kept together. It was what had made their bond so strong—they'd been all each other had had. "Is there possibly a blood relative somewhere?"

"A few, scattered here and there across the country. A great-aunt in Florida, an uncle in Chicago, a cousin in Dallas…" She crossed her arms, closing him out mentally and physically. "Just no one who wanted us."

Gently he turned her to face him. "Could he be talking about you, then?"

"Definitely not. We were in touch all during that time, but we never had a conversation about any of this."

Aidan went back to reading the entries, one of which mentioned employee hours. Copies of the schedules were attached. So was Blake keeping track of *his* alibi, or someone's whereabouts?

Blake had somehow gotten Tommy's first official reports on the arsons as well. Aidan and Kenzie discovered that he hadn't been on duty at any of the suspicious fires, a fact that Tommy had apparently considered evidence since it left Blake without an alibi for when the fires had been lit. Aidan scrolled down the list.

"Whoa, stop." Kenzie pointed to the second fire. "There. That one can't be right. He had an alibi for that one, he was with me. He'd come to Los Angeles that week. I remember because he was my date for the Emmys. He flew home immediately after, catching a red-eye because he said he had to be back at work for an early shift."

"Okay." Aidan pulled up the employee schedule for that day. "But he's not listed as on duty."

Kenzie stared at the screen, shaking her head. "He wouldn't have lied to me."

She said this with utter sincerity, and Aidan was inclined to absolutely believe because *she* believed. But if Blake *hadn't* lied to Kenzie, then there was only one other explanation.

"The schedule got changed?" she asked.

"It could have happened. Someone traded. Or—"

"Or something physically changed the schedule after the fact," she said flatly. "And Blake isn't here to defend himself."

"No, but we are." He was looking at the screen, until he realized that she wasn't. She was staring at him. "What?"

Her eyes were shimmering brilliantly with anger and something else, a deep, gut-wrenching emotion. "I didn't think it was possible." Her voice sounded thick. "I didn't want it to be possible. Oh, God." She covered her face. "This is so stupid."

"What?" He looked at the screen again, trying to figure out what she was talking about. *"What's stupid?"*

"That I could like you more than last time."

The words reached him as little had in all these years. "Kenz." Melting, he pulled down her hands. "I—"

She put a finger in his face. "Don't get excited. I

don't want to feel this way, and I'm telling you right now I *am* going to fight feeling this way."

His heart was squeezed tighter than a bow. "We were just kids, Kenz."

"And now we're not. It doesn't change anything except we're older, and *actually,* it's going to hurt more." Jaw tight, she shook her head again and looked at the screen. "This first. Blake first. He's far more important than rehashing old emotions that I don't really want to have." She worked the keyboard. "There. He's not on the schedule there, either, but he called me from the station. I know because it was my birthday, see? And he called me at 6:00 a.m. to catch me before work, but I didn't have an early morning shoot that day, and I was irritated that he woke me up. I'd been up late the night before celebrating."

"With Chad?"

She swiveled her eyes in his direction. "Actually, Teddy. Teddy White."

"Wasn't he on *People's* Most Beautiful list?"

"How do you know that?"

He knew it only because someone had stolen the porn out of the station bathroom, and Cristina had left her *People* magazine in there in its place, and— And Christ. He was crazy. "Never mind."

"It was just a one-night thing."

*Oh, great.* Even better. Now he could picture them having one-night sex, and—

"He's a friend."

A friend, as in someone who'd pulled her out of a fire? Someone who'd bail her out of jail?

"Yeah," she said softly. "I realize the word *friend* is a loose term, especially in Hollywood. Not like here."

"Do you miss it? Hollywood?"

She opened her mouth, then closed it and sighed. "I almost said yes, out of habit. The job is fun and the pay is amazing, but..." She lifted a shoulder. "It's empty. And I didn't really get that until I was here, either."

He tried to sort out his feelings regarding this revealing fact.

"And, anyway, it no longer matters." She turned back to the screen. "It's over."

"What do you mean?"

"My soap got cancelled."

"It did?"

"Yeah, and there are auditions for new parts but I've been eating too many donuts, so..."

"So...what?"

"So I'm going to get fat."

He let out a low laugh. "You look great, Kenzie. So great I haven't been able to keep my hands off you, as you might have noticed. But I'm very sorry about your job." He couldn't believe he was going to say this. "You could always stay in Santa Rey."

"I thought about it." She sighed and faced him again. "But staying seems like a comfort thing. You know, like going back to the last place where I was happy. It's a cop-out. And I was only happy here because of Blake."

He held his breath. He'd made her happy, too. Until he hadn't. "Maybe it was more than that."

"I don't know." She sighed without giving away her exact feelings on the matter, although he suspected she didn't know her exact feelings. "I wouldn't be able to get a job here."

"I know they don't film TV or movies anywhere close, but you could do something other than act."

She scoffed, then looked at him with heart-breaking hope. "Like what?"

"You know what. You could write. And eat all the damn donuts you want."

She just looked at him for a long moment, until he nearly squirmed. "What?"

"I'd have thought you'd be holding open the door for me to get the hell out of Dodge."

"Yeah, well, that was the old me."

"Well the new me is here to get Blake's name cleared. That's it."

"And also to stomp on my heart. Don't forget that part."

"I won't." She sighed. "Except I'd really rather get out of here without hurting you at all." With no idea that she'd just stunned him to his core, she leaned in close to see the screen better. A strand of her hair got stuck to the stubble on his jaw. It smelled good.

She smelled good.

It was all he could do not to bury his face in the rest

of her hair and say things that would lead her back to his bed but not really get them anywhere. In fact, he'd opened his mouth to do just that when she spoke.

"Look." She pointed to where Blake had entered another note:

*Not noted in any of the official investigation reports is the fact that the source for the wire mesh trash cans is the hardware store where Tracy works.*

Kenzie frowned and turned her head to look at Aidan, who had gone still in sudden shock. "The Tracy who…"

"Died." Aidan managed to find his vocal cords. "Yeah. They dated a couple of times. He really liked her."

"Really? He told me he'd gone out with Tracy, but he never said how much he liked her."

"Maybe he didn't tell you everything."

"He did," she insisted. "We told each other everything."

"Kenzie, you didn't tell him when *we* were going out. Maybe—"

"No." She shook her head. "You're going to say he kept secrets. That he kept the arsons a secret, but he wouldn't have— He wouldn't have done this, Aidan. Tracy being killed, well that's got to be a terrible coincidence."

"I'm beginning to believe that nothing's a coincidence. Look at the next entry."

*Tracy's going to get me a list of people who've purchased the trash cans, but she has to wait until the weekend when her boss isn't in.*

The next entry didn't clear anything up, but made it all worse.

*Got the list, and holy shit. Blood is thicker than water. Got to remember that...*

Kenzie's fingers dug into Aidan's arm. "What does that mean, 'blood *is* thicker than water'? He's written that twice now."

Aidan frowned and shook his head. "I wish I knew."

*He's onto me. Need to be damn careful now.*

"*Who's* onto him?" Kenzie stood up and paced the length of the bedroom. "God. Whoever he's talking about, do you think...?"

*Yeah.* Yeah, he did. Blake had gotten himself into hot water with someone. And that someone had either been his partner in crime, or, as Aidan was coming to believe, it was the person whom Blake had been privately, quietly, investigating on his own.

And if *that* was true, and Blake had been a victim, then this other person had not only been an arsonist, but also a murderer.

Aidan's cell phone chirped with a message that he was needed at work, ASAP.

"Go," she murmured. "It's okay. I'm just going to go through all of this and see what else I can find."

"Stay here."

Her gaze slid to his.

"Kenzie…" How to say this without sounding like a complete idiot? There was no way to sugarcoat it, so he decided to just let it out. "I have a bad feeling."

She arched an eyebrow. "You, the most pragmatic, logical, cool person I know, have a bad *feeling?*"

"Go with me on this."

"You think I'm in danger," she said flatly.

He didn't just think it, he knew it. Only he couldn't explain how or why, and that was going to drive him crazy, along with worrying and wondering where she was and if she was okay.

And safe.

And alive.

"Aidan, I'm not going to hole up here. That's ridiculous. Besides, no one knows what I'm doing."

"You were arrested, Kenzie. Everyone knows what you're doing."

"I'll be fine."

Short of tying her up, which had a *most* interesting vision popping into his head, what could he do? "Promise me you'll be careful."

She looked at him for a long moment, her hair still crazy from his fingers, her shirt crooked, her feet bare, looking like a hot mess.

A hot mess he wanted in his life.

"I thought we weren't going to do the promise thing," she said. "Not ever again."

"Promise me," he said again.

"Don't worry." She backed away from him, her face so carefully blank. "I intend to be careful and smart, and I intend to get out of here unscathed, on all counts."

What the hell did that mean?

"See you, Aidan."

Okay, that was no simple *"I'll see you later."* It seemed like a we're-done-doing-the-naked-happy-dance see-you. The get-over-me because I'm-over-you see-you.

Which didn't bode well for his heart, the one that in spite of himself, had gotten attached. Again. More attached, if that was even possible. "I'll be back."

"Okay."

"I will." He paused. "Will you be here?"

She met his gaze. "I don't know."

*Well, hell.* That didn't bode well.

# _15_

IN BETWEEN CALLS, Aidan slipped into the office of the fire station. He'd never spent much time in there, always preferring to be outside or working, or just about anywhere else.

But he made himself comfortable now. He told whoever gave him a strange look that he was working on his taxes, and given the sympathetic grimaces that got him, it was a genius excuse. Left alone, he went through the daily fire reports and employee schedules, pulling the dates that matched the arsons.

Which is where he discovered that those schedules did not match the ones Blake had saved on his computer.

In fact, according to the office reports, Blake _had_ been scheduled on each of the days of the arsons, whether by coincidence or design, Aidan had no idea. Dispatch didn't always need all available units to go out on the calls. On two of the fires, Blake's unit hadn't been called to respond at all and yet he'd been placed on scene by witnesses.

Had he been the arsonist, or simply trying to stop him?

The door to the office opened and Aidan turned around, the excuse already on his lips about being late getting his receipts together—

"Save it," Tommy said, and dropped a disk on the table.

"What's that?"

"A copy of the surveillance tape I got out of the camera I had at Blake's place."

"You had Blake's place under surveillance?"

"I'm an investigator. It's what I do, investigate."

"What were you looking for?"

"There's a bigger, better question. What was *Kenzie* looking for?"

"I couldn't tell you."

"Couldn't, or won't?"

Aidan didn't respond to that.

"You're doing a shitty job of keeping her out of my hair."

*Yeah.* He was doing a shitty job keeping Kenzie out of *his* hair as well.

"Okay, here's how this is going to work," Tommy decided. "You're going to tell me everything you've discovered about these arsons and Blake, and in return, I'm not going to charge you with interfering with my investigation."

Aidan didn't care about the underlying threat in Tommy's voice. What he cared about was discovering the truth. For Blake. For Kenzie. And as big a pain in his ass as Tommy was, Aidan believed them to be on the same side.

"Yes?"

"Yes."

With a nod, Tommy locked the door and pulled up a chair.

KENZIE HAD NO PROBLEM keeping herself occupied. She spent the day reading Blake's files, poring over them, analyzing each of her brother's entries.

She slept in Aidan's big, wonderful bed all by herself, which wasn't nearly as much fun as sleeping next to the big, wonderful man usually in it. Her dreams were wild, vacillating between nightmares about being trapped in a fire and hearing Blake scream for her, and another type of dream entirely. A dream where Aidan slowly stripped her naked and used his tongue on every inch of her body, a dream she woke up from damp with sweat, panting for air, her own hand between her thighs.

Damn, the man was potent.

In the morning, she went back to *Blake's Girl*. She couldn't help herself. She stood on the end of the dock staring at the shell that used to be Blake's sailboat, a huge lump inside her throat, wondering what the hell she was supposed to do next when her cell phone rang. Her local caller.

"Did you get the backups?"

*"Who is this?"*

"You need to stay away from the boat. There's nothing there for you."

With a gasp, she whirled, searching her immediate

area but seeing no one. "*Where are you? Are you watching me?*"

"Don't be scared."

The parking lot had only three cars in it, no people. No one was on the docks, and the neighboring boats seemed deserted. "Don't be scared? Are you crazy?"

"Listen to me," he said urgently. "It's time for you to back off. Time for you to go home, Kenzie."

The hair at the back of her neck prickled and she once again turned slowly. Behind one of the three cars was another.

Gray. Tinted windows.

Eyes narrowed, she headed toward it, needing to know who the hell she was talking to and why his voice made the hair on her arms stand up, as if she could almost recognize him, but not quite.

"Don't come any closer," he warned.

She kept walking. "Do I know you?"

The car's engine started up.

"No," she cried, breaking into a run. "*Wait—*"

The gray sedan squealed forward and to the right, giving her only the briefest glimpse of the driver behind the wheel. But it was enough to have her gasp in shock as her chest tightened beyond all bearing.

The car ripped out of the lot. She hardly even noticed as she hit her knees on the concrete, her hands fanned over her chest to hold her heart in because she'd have sworn, she'd have laid her life on the line, that the driver of that car had been none other than her dead brother.

Blake.

SHE SPED ALL THE WAY BACK to Aidan's house before remembering he was at work. Still shaken, she turned
around and headed to the station. Zach was there,
standing in the middle of the main room. He wore
jeans and a T-shirt and a rueful smile as he stuck a
pencil down the cast on his arm.

"This thing is driving me crazy." He tossed the pencil
to a small desk against a wall. "You looking for Aidan?"

"Yes." Because she wanted to tell him her brother
wasn't dead. Or that she was losing her mind. One
or the other.

"He's on a call." Zach took a closer look at her and
frowned. "Are you okay?"

*No.* "I saw the file you put together on the arsons."
The fires had cost Zach his house, which in itself
would have given him a good reason to hate her
brother. "When Blake died, there wasn't a body."

A shadow crossed his face. "The fire was hot.
Nothing survived it."

She begged to differ. "Anything survive? Anything at all?"

"A portion of the shell of the blow torch Blake had
been holding, and his hard hat."

"But no physical evidence of *him?*"

He paused a long moment. "Why?"

*Oh, because maybe he hadn't really died...* "Do
you know when Aidan'll be back?"

"No, but I can have him call you. He was worried
about you."

"I'm fine." She smiled to prove it, but truthfully, she was worried, too. She left the station, got into her car and pulled out her cell. Taking a deep breath, she dialed her mysterious caller's number.

"Hello."

Kenzie went utterly still at that voice, still disguised, but it didn't matter. She now knew who she was talking to. "Blake?"

*Click.*

*Oh, God.* Heart pounding, she drove straight to Tommy Ramirez's office. He opened his door at her knock, raising a single eyebrow at the sight of her, then simply sighed when she pushed past him and let herself in.

He had three unopened Red Bulls on his desk. She grabbed one, cracked it open and drank deeply. Eyes closed, she stood there until the caffeine kicked in. "God, I needed that."

He shut the door, leaned back against it and just looked at her. "That was my Red Bull."

"Thanks for sharing."

"You know, most people are afraid of me."

"Yes, but most people don't know that once upon a time you paid for my dancing lessons."

"Keep it down, will you? I don't want that to get out."

She shook her head. "Always the tough guy." Back when Blake had been in the academy, she and her brother had made some financial mistakes. Lots of financial mistakes. Tommy had known Blake's situation and had lent him some money to see him through fire school, and Kenzie enough to cover her dance lessons.

Not many knew the investigator had such a soft side; he didn't like to show it. He hadn't shown it to Kenzie since, but she'd never forgotten. Nor had she ever even briefly considered that it could be Tommy framing Blake. Blake had trusted Tommy, and she did, too.

Tommy tossed the files in his hands to his desk and grabbed one of the remaining Red Bulls. "I put you in jail to keep you safe. I didn't intend for you to bail yourself out. I wanted to keep you there until this was over, but it's taking longer than I thought."

"You put me in jail to keep me safe?"

"Trust me, it made sense to me. Look, I know this has been hard on you."

"Yes," she agreed blandly. "It's been hard on me having my brother blamed for something he didn't do. It's been hard on me knowing that all his friends, his coworkers, *everyone,* believes he committed arson. It's hard on me knowing that he can't defend himself. But it's even harder knowing that you're not."

"You don't understand."

"Then help me to."

He opened his mouth, and then shut it. "I can't."

"Would you like to know what the hardest thing of all is?" she whispered, her throat tight with a sudden need to cry. "I know he's innocent and I know that you believe it, too."

"Kenzie—"

"You can't talk about it, I get it. But I think I saw Blake alive. Can you talk about that?"

He stared at her. *"What?"*

"I think I saw him at the docks, in the parking lot."

Tommy sank to his chair. "What were you doing at the docks?"

"Blake. *Alive.* Did you hear that part?"

His eyes filled with sympathy. "Kenzie—"

"No." She let out a low laugh. "Listen to me. *I saw him.* Plus someone's been calling me, giving me clues. It's him, he—"

"What kind of clues?"

"I don't know, that the key is in the demos, which I don't get. And that blood is thicker than water. I don't get that either, honestly."

Tommy went pale. He came to her, taking her arm and leading her to the door. "I need you to listen to me, okay? Listen very carefully. Go back to Los Angeles. I'll call you—"

"No." She pulled free. "I'm not leaving."

"Yes, you are. If I have to have you arrested again—"

"On what charges?"

"I'll find something."

She looked into his face, where his emotions were clear. "Okay, you're scared for me. I get that. I'll stay back, I'll stay clear."

*"Promise me."*

She took a long look at him. "What did I say? Was it the blood is thicker than water thing?"

"Promise me."

"I promise," she said very quietly. "Now you promise me this. You'll come to me as soon as you can with answers."

"Deal."

DURING THE SUMMER MONTHS, Santa Rey swelled to upwards of three times its normal population, which was reflected in the increased volume of calls the fire station received. In the past twenty-four hours alone, Aidan had fought a restaurant fire, a storefront fire, a car fire and two house fires, each caused by human stupidity. Then, it happened.

Another explosion.

It thankfully occurred in an empty warehouse this time. No one was injured, except Cristina, who fell off a ladder and hurt her ankle.

Dustin wanted to take her to the E.R. for an X-ray, but in typical Cristina fashion, she wanted to tough it out.

Aidan left them alone to their silent battle of wills, and let himself inside the burned shell of a warehouse.

Tommy was there, with his bag of equipment, his camera out. When he saw Aidan, he jaw ticked. "I've got it from here."

Aidan's eyes went to the wall in front of Tommy, where the burn marks on the wall indicated a hot flash, and most likely, the point of origin. "I never did get onto *Blake's Girl* after the explosion. But I'm going to take a wild guess that you found something like this there, and also at the hardware explosion that killed Tracy."

Tommy clearly fought with himself, and then finally sighed. "Look, I'm not going to insult your intelligence the way I insulted Zach's, okay? That was a mistake, shutting him out, because it only made him all the more determined to prove he was right—"

"He *was* right—"

"Yeah, but I was on it. I told him that, but he didn't listen, and then he dug harder and got himself targeted by the arsonist."

"The arsonist? I thought you were so sure it was Blake."

"I'm not going to insult your intelligence," he repeated tightly, "by letting you think what we want the general public to think. So know this. I'm going to nail this guy. So when I say back off, *do it*. Don't pull a Zach and get yourself hurt."

Aidan stared at him. "You know there's someone else."

"I'm close."

"You've always known."

Tommy acknowledged this with a slight nod. "So now all you have to do is stay out of my way. And keep Kenzie out of the way as well. No one else dies."

"Blake's innocent."

"That's one theory."

"Is it the right theory?"

"Jesus, Aidan." Tommy scrubbed a hand over his face. "Are you just playing with that girl?"

"No. And how is this any of your business, anyway? A few days ago you were arresting her."

"Just don't hurt her. You hear me? Don't even think about it."

Aidan let out a low, mirthless laugh. "Trust me, if someone's getting hurt, it's going to be me."

THE MINUTE AIDAN GOT OFF WORK, he went straight home, hoping Kenzie would be there waiting for him. It was with great relief that he pulled in next to her car. Letting himself in, he called out her name.

No response. Dropping his keys on the small desk in the living room, he moved through the house and heard the shower running. Things were looking up if he had a naked, wet, hot woman in his shower. And at that realization, all the myriad things he'd wanted to say to her flew out the window, replaced by memories of how she looked standing under a stream of water.

She hadn't left…

Weak with relief, he knocked on the bathroom door. "Kenz?"

When she still didn't respond, he cracked open the door and found her sitting in his shower, face to her knees, arms wrapped around herself.

"Kenzie?"

"I'm fine."

*Yeah.* She was fine, he was fine, so they could just all be fine together.

She lifted her head when he opened the shower door but didn't say a word as he stepped into it with her.

"You're dressed," she finally said, inanely.

Yeah, which sucked. "Tell me what's wrong."

"You're not going to like it."

He already didn't like it, or the clothes now sticking to him like a second skin. "Try me."

"I saw Blake."

He blinked away the water in his eyes. "You…saw Blake." He crouched before her. "In a dream?"

"No."

"You saw Blake," he repeated, trying to understand, and failing. "Not in a dream. What does that mean?"

"It means he's alive."

# 16

Kenzie watched Aidan try to absorb her news while the shower rained down over top of him, soaking into his hair, his clothes. "I know, it's a shock," she said.

The water ran in rivulets down his face. His shirt was plastered to his broad shoulders and arms, his pants suctioned to his legs. There was something about the way he'd rushed in there to save her from her own demons that got to her. More than got to her. He devastated her.

She wasn't sure how it'd happened, especially when she'd set out to keep her heart safe, but she'd fallen for him all over again.

"You saw Blake," he repeated.

"He's alive. He's the one who's been calling me." She stood up. "He's been alive and didn't tell me. The men I love suck."

Aidan hissed out a breath and straightened to his feet as well, towering over her, his broad shoulders taking the beating of the water. "The men you love?"

"Go away."

"The men you love?" he asked, staring down at her. "Kenz—"

"No." She shook her head. "Not doing this." She put her hands on his chest to shove him away but somehow ended up fisting her hands in his drenched shirt and yanking. Surprised, he lost his balance as he came toward her, slapping his hands on the tile on either side of her to hold himself upright. "Kenz—"

She stopped whatever he might have said with her mouth. It made no sense, none at all, but she wanted to have him, needed to have him, right there, right then, if only for this one last time before all hell broke loose.

*"God,"* he managed on a roughly expelled breath as she kissed her way over his jaw while she fumbled with the buttons on his Levi's.

His hands left the tile and squeezed her arms. Water was running down his face. "I thought you'd said good-bye to me."

She'd tried. After all, she had a life to get back to. Too bad she had no idea what that life would entail— but that was a worry for tomorrow. After she figured out the Blake being alive thing. "So I said good-bye. Now I'm saying hello." Still squished between the wall and Aidan, she slid her hands up his chest, her fingers entwining in his hair as she arched back, her breasts sliding along the material of his wet shirt.

Her nipples hardened and she felt the rough grumble of the groan in his chest. Almost as if acting of their own accord, his hands moved down her sides, to her hips, her bottom, which he roughly squeezed while letting out another of those incredibly arousing groans. "Is there another good-bye coming my way after this shower?"

"Maybe not right after," she panted because something was happening to her, something that had nothing to do with lust or hormones or getting an orgasm, but far deeper. Far more dangerous. Tightening her fingers in his hair, she lifted his head from her breast and stared into his eyes. There, she could see the reflection of her own. And in that reflection was her heart and soul, her very life.

She loved him. And if they did this, if she let him inside her body again, she'd never recover. She knew it, but like last time, it wasn't going to stop her. Small wonder when he was against her like a second skin, holding her to the wall. Closing her eyes, she hugged him close, pressing her face to his throat.

Her name tumbled from his lips in a harsh whisper, and then their hands were fighting to get his clothes off, pushing off his shirt, shoving down his jeans. Then he was reaching for those jeans, and the condom in his pocket. He pressed her back against the wall, freeing his hands to skim down her bare, trembling thighs, which opened and wrapped around his waist, bringing him flush to her. In one thrust he was deep inside, and she was…lost?

Not lost.

No, when she was with him, she was found.

AIDAN'S HEART was still thundering in his ears in tune to the water pounding his back when Kenzie slid free of him. Drained, he watched her lean past him and turn off the water. She tossed him a towel, grabbed one for herself and left him alone in the bathroom.

He had no idea what had just happened.

When he managed to dry himself off and walk out of the bathroom, on legs that still quivered, he found her dressing in his bedroom. "Did you get the license of that truck that just hit me?"

She didn't smile. "I really saw him."

When he just looked at her, she slipped into her shoes. "And I'm going to go find him."

"Kenzie," he said gently. "Blake is—"

"Dead. I know. But he's not." She left the room.

With a sigh, he headed to his dresser for clothes. He'd gotten into a dry pair of jeans when he heard her keys jangling. "Kenzie," he called out. *Dammit.* "Wait." He grabbed a shirt and headed down the hallway just as she opened the front door. She hesitated when her cell phone beeped an incoming text message.

"Is it…him?" he asked.

"Yes, it's him. Texting me from the dead." She opened her phone and let him read over her shoulder.

*Go home. I'll find you there when this is over, when you're safe.*

As they stood there in his open doorway looking down at the screen, a huge trash truck lumbered down the street, making the earth shudder as it went past—
*Boom.*

Kenzie's bright red sports car vanished in a cloud of smoke and flames and flying metal as it exploded.

KENZIE SAT ON AIDAN'S CURB looking out at the street, which was littered with cops and various other official personnel, including Tommy and the chief. And lots of red car parts.

Everyone was trying to figure out what the hell had happened.

Her car had gone boom, just like *Blake's Girl,* that was what had happened.

"Kenzie." Aidan's athletic shoes appeared in her peripheral vision, and then the rest of him as he sat at her side.

"My insurance company isn't going to be happy," she said. "I blame the trash truck."

"The trash truck saved your life. You car had been rigged to blow when you got into it, but the truck vibrated the street so much it went up early."

"Oh." She winced. "I wish I didn't know that."

"Give me your cell phone."

"Why?"

"So I can call whoever's been calling you."

"Blake. Blake's been calling me."

"Whoever it is." His mouth was grim as some of his clear frustration and fear for her filtered into his words. "I just want him to stay the hell away from you."

"This wasn't him."

"Then who?"

"I'm working on that."

He looked down at her. "By yourself."

"It's how I work best, apparently." She stood up. During the time she'd been gone from Santa Rey, she'd closed herself off, both her heart and soul. It was a hell of a time to realize that. But no matter what happened here—whether she left and went back to Los Angeles, or whether she stayed—whatever she settled on for herself, she couldn't go back to closing herself off.

"Kenzie."

"I didn't mean to get so good at being alone. I didn't realize, living in L.A., the land of pretend, that I'd never built myself any real relationships." She let out a long breath and met his gaze. "But that changed when I got here. When I was with you. I love you, Aidan. Again. Still. I love you."

And while that shocking statement hung in the air, someone called for Aidan. But he just stared at Kenzie. "You—"

"Aidan!"

With a grimace, he looked over his shoulder. "Shit, it's the chief."

"Go."

"Kenzie—"

"*Go.*"

A muscle ticked in his jaw. "Don't move, I'll be right back."

Nodding, she watched him walk toward a tall man whose back was to her, stretching out a dark blue shirt that said Chief across the shoulders.

Then she walked away. She didn't have a car, so she had no idea where she thought she was going, but she had to leave.

In her pocket, her cell phone buzzed with an incoming text.

*Another half block. Gray car.*

I LOVE YOU. Aidan muttered the three little words that Kenzie had said to him. She'd said them, and then she'd vanished, and he had no idea where she'd gone. One moment he'd been talking to the chief, and the next… She'd been gone. It'd been hours, and not a word.

He was at the station now, and she still hadn't answered her damn cell phone, and he was starting to lose it. He shouldn't have walked away to talk to the chief, he should have dragged her with him.

"Hey, Mr. 2008." Cristina came into the station kitchen and went straight for the refrigerator. "What are you pouting about?" She helped herself to someone else's lunch.

"You could bring your own."

"I could." Cristina pulled out a thick turkey sandwich. "But I don't."

"Hey, that's mine," Dustin said, joining them from the garage. "What did I tell you about stealing my sandwich?"

Cristina spoke around a huge mouthful. "If I was still sleeping with you, I'd bet you'd *give* me your sandwich."

Dustin's eyes darkened. "You slept with me once."

"Your point?"

"My point is that if we were *still* sleeping together, I'd *make* you your own damn sandwich."

She took another bite, chewing with a moan. "You know, I should give that some thought, because you do make the best sandwiches."

Dustin tossed up his hands and walked back out of the room.

When he was gone, Cristina dropped her tough girl pose, watching him go with a naked look of longing.

"You could just tell him the truth," Aidan said.

"What, that he makes crappy sandwiches?"

"No, that you're scared. He'd understand fear." Hell, he understood it all too well.

"Are you kidding me? I'm not scared." Cristina tossed the sandwich back in the fridge. "I'm not scared of anything." But as she shut the fridge, she pressed her forehead to the door. "Ah, hell. I'm scared. Everything's messed up. Dustin's mad at me. Blake's gone. There's no good food. Blake's gone."

"You still miss him."

"Hell, yeah, I still miss him. He was a great partner. And now even the chief, his own flesh and blood, wants to make him out to be a monster that we know he wasn't."

"Wait." Aidan grabbed her arm. "What?"

"He wasn't a monster."

"The flesh and blood part. What did you mean about that?"

Cristina's lips tightened. "Blake asked me never to tell."

"He asked you never to tell what?"

She sighed. "That the chief's his uncle. They were estranged, though. Blake's parents were—"

"Dead. They died years ago."

"Yeah. But his father was the chief's half brother."

*Blood is thicker than water… Good God.* "If that's true," he asked hoarsely, "why did Blake and Kenzie spend their childhood in foster care?"

"Because the chief didn't want kids. Or something like that." She shrugged. "Not sure on the details."

Neither was he. Except that somehow…*Christ.* Somehow the chief—

His cell phone rang. When he looked down at the screen, his heart skipped a beat. "Thank God," he said to Kenzie in lieu of a greeting. "Listen to me. I just realized—"

"Aidan, I need you. I'm sorry, I know I don't really have the right to say that to you, but I do. Can you come meet me? Now? Please?"

"Just tell me where."

AIDAN BURST INSIDE the Sunrise Café and looked around the tables.

No Kenzie.

"She's on the roof," Sheila told him, standing behind the bar drying glasses.

"Thanks."

"Something about Tommy being on his way, and having all the answers you need…"

*Aidan* had the answers. He just didn't have the girl,

which he intended to rectify. He headed for the stairs as Sheila turned her attention to someone else. "Hey, there, good-looking," she called out with a smile of greeting. Aidan took the stairs without looking back, coming to a relieved halt on the roof at the sight of Kenzie sitting on the bench.

"Tommy's on his way," she said, standing up. Someone stepped out from the shadows behind her and Aidan's heart stopped.

It was Blake, who by all logical accounts should be dead.

Only there was nothing logical about any of this. Not the arsons, and not the way Aidan knew he loved the woman standing in front of him like he'd never loved anyone before.

"Listen to him," Kenzie said quietly. "Listen to your heart."

He *was* listening to his heart, which had kicked back to life and was screaming, demanding that he pull Kenzie close and tell her he loved her, too. That he was sorry it'd taken him so long, but like Cristina, he'd been afraid, was in fact *still* afraid but would no longer run from how he felt.

He'd never again run from her.

But that would have to wait. He looked at Blake, who was thinner than ever. And he walked with a cane. "I know, it's crazy," his old friend said, his voice low and urgent. "You thought I was dead and I'm not. I…faked my own death."

"I'm getting that."

"When I found out who the real arsonist was, I realized no one was safe." Blake's face was twisted in tortured misery. "He killed Tracy right after he blew up my boat."

"I know. I know all of it. I even know *who* we're talking about. I just don't know why."

"Oh, I can tell you why," said the man who came through the roof door to stand in front of them. The chief nodded in Aidan's direction. "If you really want to know."

*Shit.* Aidan pulled out his cell, hit Tommy's number and put the phone to his ear.

"Nearly there," Tommy said tensely.

"Hurry. Bring backup."

"Oh, it'll be too late," the chief said conversationally.

"Uncle Allan?" Kenzie breathed, staring at the chief. She looked at Aidan. "He's the fire chief? I thought…" She turned back to her uncle. "I thought you were in Chicago."

"I was. I came back here a year ago. A shame we lost touch or you'd have known."

"We lost touch—" Kenzie took a step toward him, or tried to, but Blake grabbed her hand and held her back "—because you didn't want us."

"Now, now. That's not entirely true. I just didn't want to be responsible for raising kids. I never wanted kids."

"But it's okay to be responsible for *killing people?*"

"*One* person," he corrected. "Not people. And that was an accident."

"You killed Tracy and that was no accident," Blake ground out. "You murdered her."

"Ah, now, see *murder* implies intent, and I don't have intent. I have an addiction." He smiled sadly. "It means I can't help it."

Kenzie again tried to charge him, but this time it was Aidan who held her back, not trusting that asshole with her.

"If I was an alcoholic," the chief asked, "would you still be looking at me like that? If I had a drug problem? No, you'd be trying to get me help."

"I *tried* to get you help," Blake told him. "When I figured out you had started that second fire all those months ago, you begged me to understand. You lied and said it was your first time, and that you'd stop, that you'd get help. Instead a child died and when I tried to turn you in you threatened me."

The chief slowly shook his head. "Tommy was getting close. You wouldn't leave me alone. I had to do something. I had to keep you quiet."

Blake gave Aidan an agonized look, as though pleading for forgiveness. "By then he had implicated me. He'd changed the schedules, he'd planted evidence. He discredited me so that even if I did tell, *I'd* be the first one they'd lock up. And once I was in jail, he threatened to hurt Kenzie.

"Then Zach started asking questions and the chief tried to kill him by burning down his house. I had followed him, Zach saw me, and I didn't know what to do. I panicked and faked my death. If I was gone, he had no reason to harm Kenzie."

"And I didn't."

"You killed Tracy!"

"But not Kenzie," the chief said calmly. "Look, Tracy was going to put together a list of people who'd purchased those metal trash cans. I would have been on that list."

"You didn't have to kill her," Blake shouted.

"He had to set more fires," Aidan said grimly.

"That's true." The chief nodded emphatically. "I can't help myself. I tried like hell. I couldn't stop, but at least I went for old and dilapidated properties, or overly insured buildings." He paused. "Like this one."

Aidan stared at him. "What?"

"Sheila is getting ready to renovate," the chief said.

"She has to," Aidan said. "The building has structural problems."

"Yes, and now she's over insured to protect it. It's a situation that cries out to an arsonist. It needs to burn."

"Ohmigod," Kenzie breathed, looking horrified. "You're a very sick man."

"Agreed." Her uncle smiled without any mirth. He clapped his hands together. "Well, it's been nice clearing all this up but I've got to end this now."

"You're not walking away," Aidan said. "Not from this. You have to pay for your crimes."

"I'm not paying for anything. You didn't get hurt. None of you died."

"Are you kidding?" Aidan asked incredulously. "Blake nearly died trying to stop you. You nearly killed Kenzie on *Blake's Girl,* and then again when you blew up her car."

"*Nearly* won't hold up in a court of law. I was just trying to scare her out of town, anyway. The car was supposed to blow an hour earlier, but a fuse failed me. And the boat was an accident. I was just trying to get rid of Blake's laptop. I didn't know she was there that night."

"There's something else you don't know," Aidan told him. "Blake e-mailed Kenzie backup files."

The chief's mouth tightened. "I'm not going down for this, for any of it. I'm the chief."

"Not for long you're not," Blake said. "You're going to be stripped of that title and put in jail."

"Not happening," the Chief declared. "I won't go to jail—I've made sure of it. I've risked my life to save people for almost thirty years. I *won't* be remembered as an arsonist."

Aidan's gut clenched. There was only one reason the chief would come out in the open like this and confess his crimes. And that was if he didn't intend for them to live to tell the tale. "Whatever you've planned, *no*."

"You're too late." The chief looked first to Kenzie, then to Blake. "I'm sorry. Truly sorry."

"What did you do?" Blake demanded. "Oh, Christ, you didn't—" Without finishing that thought, he whirled and limped to the roof door, yelling as he took the stairs, "Evacuate! Everyone out—"

Which was all he got out before a thundering explosion hit. The entire building shook, throwing Aidan and Kenzie to the ground.

# 17

AT THE EXPLOSION, the world seemed to stop, or at least go into slow motion. Kenzie managed to lift her head just as Aidan rolled toward her, his face a mask of concern. Her uncle, ten feet away, wasn't moving at all. Pushing to her knees, she stared at the doorway where her brother had just disappeared. "Blake!" she screamed.

He didn't reappear, no one did, nothing except a plume of smoke that struck terror in her heart. "Ohmigod. *Aidan*—"

"Are you okay?" He was on his knees before her, running his hands down her sides, pushing her hair from her face, looking her over, his expression calm, only his eyes showing his fear. "Are you okay?" he demanded again hoarsely.

Shaken, but all in one piece, she nodded and pointed to the doorway. "Blake—"

His eyes and mouth were grim. "I know. He's down with the others. We'll get to him." He glanced at the chief.

"Is he—"

Aidan checked for a pulse. "Just out cold." He

pulled her to her feet, yanking his cell phone out of his pocket. From far below, they could hear screams and yelling over the whooping sound of smoke and car alarms going off.

All of it brought Kenzie back to the night on *Blake's Girl,* back to that irrational terror. Then they'd been able to jump into the water. Now there was nothing down there except concrete.

Three floors down.

"Call 9-1-1," Aidan said to her, shoving the phone into her hands as he ran past the very still chief to the edge of the building and looked over the side. "Dammit, I can't see if people are getting out of here."

The café hadn't been full to capacity, but there had been at least twenty people inside when they'd entered, and then there was Sheila and her staff.

And Blake. God, Blake. Could she really have found him only to lose him again, for real this time? "Aidan—"

"Listen to me. There's no way off of here except for the stairwell. No outside fire escape or ladder."

They both looked at the dark doorway, emitting smoke now. "Ohmigod." She felt frozen. Logically she knew she had to go down to get to Blake, not to mention to safety. But there was nothing logical about the fear blocking her windpipe. She'd thought Blake had died in a fire. *She'd* nearly died in the boat fire. Instead of seeing the roof's doorway, she kept flashing back to *Blake's Girl,* the black night and blacker water. She could feel the heat from that fire prickling her skin even as she could feel the iciness of the water closing around her body—

"Kenzie."

She blinked Aidan into view. He had his hands on her arms and he was frowning into her face.

"I can't go in there," she said, unable to catch her breath. "I just can't."

"Okay." They both looked at the chief, who still wasn't moving. Again Aidan went to the edge of the roof and looked over. Whatever he saw made his jaw go tight and his eyes, grim. Then he backed Kenzie to a corner and gently pushed her down until she was sitting there, her back to the wall, facing the opened door to the only exit. "I'm going—"

"No." She gripped his arms, digging her fingers into the muscles there.

"Kenzie—"

"No!" Icy, terrifying fear overcame her as she stared at the smoke now pouring out through the opened door. "There's a fire down there!"

He didn't say it, he didn't have to.

"I already hear sirens. They're coming to put out the fire. It's going to be okay. But I have to go help. This roof won't be safe to be on for long."

"I know."

With his eyes reflecting the torment he felt at leaving her, he pried her fingers from his arms.

"Come right back," she ordered.

"Okay."

"And stay safe, you hear me?"

"I will."

"And Blake. Bring me Blake."

"I promise." He held her gaze for one beat, letting her see into his heart and soul. He never made promises, never, and yet he did now, to her, which meant more than anything he'd ever done. Pretending to be brave, she nodded and then sagged back, covering her face with her hands so she couldn't see the smoke pouring out of the doorway as he vanished into it.

Dammit, she really needed a new script. Aidan was probably worrying about her instead of completely focusing on the fire—and that was dangerous. She forced her eyes open, glued her gaze to the black doorway. He had saved her life on Blake's boat, and that had been amazing, but she could have saved herself. She knew how to swim.

And she could save herself this time.

All she had to do was get past her fear. Any second now…

The sirens were louder now, and that reached her somehow. Tommy was probably nearly here, too. She got to her feet, wiped the sweat from her eyes and headed to her uncle. He'd hit his head on the A/C vent. Turning her back on him, she headed toward the door. "You're a coward," she told herself. "You're fine, you're fine…" She kept up the mantra as she entered the dark doorway. Unable to breathe through the smoke, she pulled her shirt up over her mouth and took another step.

And then it happened. The floor beneath her rumbled, the walls shimmied and shook, and she froze as a second explosion hit, flinging her against a wall. Then the power flickered and went off, leaving her in complete darkness.

*Oh, God.*

Sitting up, she felt for the railing and pushed herself upright. She was okay. Relatively speaking, anyway.

Just as she began heading down again, the stairs beneath her began rumbling, but not with yet another explosion. This time it was pounding footsteps as someone ran up the stairs, and then reached out toward her. "Kenzie?"

"*Blake?* Ohmigod, Blake, you're okay—"

"Where is he? The chief?" he demanded.

"On the roof."

"Stay here," he commanded. "Stay right here!" And then he rushed up and out.

*Like hell.* She was going to be proactive this time, dammit. She was rewriting this script her way. And when it was over, she was going to write scripts all damn day long to her heart's content. And eat donuts. Yeah, lots of donuts. Heart pounding, she stumbled after her brother. Bursting back out on the roof, she was horrified to see that part of it had begun to cave in, with flames flickering out from underneath. And standing far too close to that area was Blake, facing off with the chief.

"No," she cried, just as Aidan came out the doorway behind her, looking as if he'd been in a car wreck, all torn and bloody, calling her name hoarsely.

"You're hurt," she cried, rushing to his side.

"The explosion kicked me down the stairs." He

hugged her tight, not taking his eyes off the chief and Blake. "I'm okay."

It was like a bad movie, playing in slow motion as the chief leaped for the edge of the roof, and Blake leaped for him the best he could, wrestling him to the ground.

Flames shot up through the floor at all of them and Kenzie screamed, trying to get close to her brother, but Aidan had a hold of her, even though *he* was the one with torn clothing and blood seeping from his various injuries, all covered in soot.

On the ground now, Blake rolled with the chief, the two of them still throwing punches.

"Stay back," Aidan told her, holding onto her. "The flames—"

They were licking at them from all angles now, but suddenly, from below, they were hit with water. Streams of it, coming up from the street.

The fire trucks had arrived, and none too soon as the flames forced Kenzie and Aidan back from yet another cave-in.

"Hold still, you son of a bitch," Blake growled out to the chief, who was trying to crawl free and get to the edge of the roof.

Aidan tried to move around the flames to help Blake with the chief, but suddenly he wavered, then sank to his knees.

"Aidan!"

"Yeah. Think maybe I hit my head before." He blinked at her face as she dropped to her knees in front of him. "There's three of you."

"Oh, God." She touched the gash along his temple, which was bleeding freely. "Hold still!"

"Not a problem."

A ladder and bucket came into view over the roofline, lifted by a crane from below. It held two fire-fighters, who took one look at Blake and staggered to a shocked halt.

"Later," Blake yelled at them. "I'll explain later! Aidan's down and we need Tommy and some cuffs. Tell me someone has some cuffs!"

IT ACTUALLY WASN'T THAT EASY, nothing ever was, Kenzie thought. Hours later, they were all sitting around Aidan's hospital bed, where he was being held overnight, thanks to a concussion.

The chief had been taken to jail, which was such a huge town scandal that Tommy had left to prepare for a press conference. Sheila was sitting in a chair, her wrist in a sling. It was her only injury, but the café was a complete loss. Dustin was next to her, his arm around her shoulders. Cristina was there, too, holding a bucket full of money from emergency personnel on the scene who'd already poured some of their support into it for Sheila.

"I could go to Hawaii with all that." Tears were thick in Sheila's voice.

"Or you could rebuild," Aidan said from flat on his back.

At the sound of his voice, Kenzie's heart squeezed. He'd been so damn quiet, and she'd been so damn worried.

On the other side of Aidan's bed, Blake stirred. "The chief's in custody," he told Aidan. "And he's not going to get off easy."

Aidan's gaze tracked to Kenzie. "I don't want to get off easy, either." He reached for her hand. "Not tonight, or any night."

She gripped his fingers tightly and pressed them to her aching heart. He was talking, but not making any sense. She hadn't taken a full breath since they'd taken him for X-rays and she didn't take one now. "I'll go get your nurse—"

"No." His grip was like iron. "I'm not crazy."

"I know—"

"Listen to me. You pulled it off, you broke my damn heart. We're even."

Oh, God, and now he was delirious. "Aidan—"

"Maybe we should give them a moment," Dustin said, guiding Sheila out of the room. Cristina followed.

Blake did not leave. "What's going on?"

"I love you back, Kenzie." Aidan managed a smile, although it was crooked. "But I think you already knew that."

"No." She shook her head, finding herself both laughing and crying. "I didn't. I hoped…"

Blake was staring at the two of them, mouth grim. "Wait. Love?"

Aidan, who still hadn't stopped looking into Kenzie's eyes, nodded. "Definitely love."

And just like that, Kenzie took a full breath. God, it felt good to breathe. Breathe and live and love.

"Okay, somebody talk to me," Blake said.

"Well you've been dead, or I'd have told you before now," Kenzie reminded him. "I've been busy trying to make Aidan pay for breaking my heart all those years ago."

At this, Blake blinked, then sent a glacial stare at Aidan. "You broke my sister's heart?"

Aidan winced. "Yeah, but if it helps, I was an idiot."

"He really was," Kenzie agreed.

"And trust me, she got me back," Aidan said. "Her evil plan worked. I fell hard. I love her, Blake." He broke eye contact with Kenzie and looked right at Blake, his smile gone, eyes dead serious. "I love her with everything I've got."

Blake looked as if a good wind could knock him over. "You put your heart out there? *You?*"

Bringing his and Kenzie's still joined hands to his chest, Aidan nodded. "Yeah."

"And then she stomped on it?"

"In boots, with spikes on the soles," Aidan assured him.

Blake took this in and considered, then relaxed. "Okay, then. As long as you're even."

"Not even," Kenzie whispered. "Not yet."

Uncertainty twisted Aidan's features. "Kenzie—"

"We're not even until I get my happily-ever-after." Her throat was so tight she could barely speak. "But since I'm going to be writing, I'm pretty sure I can plot it out for myself."

Aidan's eyes registered both surprise and pride.

"You're going to be great at writing. But about that ending… Am I in it?"

"I can guarantee it."

He smiled, and right then, Kenzie knew. She didn't need a script for this, her life, not anymore. The real thing was so much better. Taking the first step, she cupped Aidan's gorgeous face and kissed him.

\* \* \* \* \*

*Wait! It's not over yet! Dustin and Cristina*
*still have some unfinished business to attend to.*
*Find out how they, uh, work out their differences in*
*the upcoming* BLAZE *Christmas anthology:*
*HEATING UP THE HOLIDAYS by Jill Shalvis,*
*Jacquie D'Alessandro and Jamie Sobrato.*
*Available in December 2008.*

*The Colton family is back!*
*Enjoy a sneak preview of*
*COLTON'S SECRET SERVICE*
*by Marie Ferrarella, part of*
THE COLTONS: FAMILY FIRST *miniseries.*
*Available from Silhouette Romantic Suspense*
*in September 2008.*

He cautioned himself to be leery. He was human and he'd been conned before. But never by anyone nearly so attractive. Never by anyone he'd felt so attracted to.

In her defense, Nick supposed that Georgie could actually be telling him the truth. That she was a victim in all this. He had his people back in California checking her out, to make sure she was who she said she was and had, as she claimed, not even been near a computer but on the road these last few months that the threats had been made.

In the meantime, he was doing his own checking out. Up close and exceedingly personal. So personal he could feel his blood stirring.

It had been a long time since he'd thought of himself

as anything other than a law enforcement agent of one type or other. But Georgeann Grady made him remember that beneath the oaths he had taken and his devotion to duty, there beat the heart of a man.

A man who'd been far too long without the touch of a woman.

He watched as the light from the fireplace caressed the outline of Georgie's small, trim, jean-clad body as she moved about the rustic living room that could have easily come off the set of a Hollywood Western. Except that it was genuine.

As genuine as she claimed to be?

Something inside of him hoped so.

He wasn't supposed to be taking sides. His only interest in being here was to guarantee Senator Joe Colton's safety as the latter continued to make his bid for the presidency. Everything else was supposed to be secondary, but, Nick had to silently admit, that was just a wee bit hard to remember right now.

Earlier, before she'd put her precocious handful of a daughter to bed, Georgie had fed his appetite by whipping up some kind of a delicious concoction out of the vegetables she'd pulled from her garden. Vegetables that, by all rights, should have been withered and dried. She'd mentioned that a friend came by on occasion to weed and tend it. Still, it surprised him that somehow she'd managed to make something mouth-watering out of it.

Almost as mouthwatering as she looked to him right at this moment.

Again, he was reminded of the appetite that hadn't been fed, hadn't been satisfied.

And wasn't going to be, Nick sternly told himself. At least not now. Maybe later, when things took on a more definite shape and all the questions in his head were answered to his satisfaction, there would be time to explore this feeling. This woman. But not now.

Damn it.

"Sorry about the lack of light," Georgie said, breaking into his train of thought as she turned around to face him. If she noticed the way he was looking at her, she gave no indication. "But I don't see a point in paying for electricity if I'm not going to be here. Besides, Emmie really enjoys camping out. She likes roughing it."

"And you?" Nick asked, moving closer to her, so close that a whisper would have trouble fitting in. "What do you like?"

The very breath stopped in Georgie's throat as she looked up at him.

"I think you've got a fair shot of guessing that one," she told him softly.

\* \* \* \* \*

*Be sure to look for COLTON'S SECRET SERVICE*
*and the other following titles from*
THE COLTONS: FAMILY FIRST *miniseries:*
*RANCHER'S REDEMPTION by Beth Cornelison*
*THE SHERIFF'S AMNESIAC BRIDE*
*by Linda Conrad*
*SOLDIER'S SECRET CHILD by Caridad Piñeiro*
*BABY'S WATCH by Justine Davis*
*A HERO OF HER OWN by Carla Cassidy*

## The Coltons Are Back!

# Marie Ferrarella
## *Colton's Secret Service*

### The Coltons: Family First

On a mission to protect a senator, Secret Service agent
Nick Sheffield tracks down a threatening message only
to discover Georgie Gradie Colton, a rodeo-riding single
mom, who insists on her innocence. Nick is instantly
taken with the feisty redhead, but vows not to let his
feelings interfere with his mission. Now he must figure
out if this woman is conning him or if he can trust her
and the passion they share....

**Available September wherever books are sold.**

**Visit Silhouette Books at www.eHarlequin.com**  SRS27598

# REQUEST YOUR FREE BOOKS!

## 2 FREE NOVELS
## PLUS 2
## FREE GIFTS!

**Red-hot reads!**

HB08R

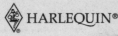

# COMING NEXT MONTH

### #417 ALL OR NOTHING  Debbi Rawlins
Posing undercover as a Hollywood producer to investigate thefts at the
St. Martine hotel has good ol' Texas cowboy Chase Culver sweatin' under
his Stetson. All the up-close contact with the hotel's gorgeous personal trainer
Dana McGuire isn't helping either, and she's his prime suspect!

### #418 RISQUÉ BUSINESS  Tawny Weber
*Blush*
Delaney Connor can't believe the way her life has changed! The former mousy
college professor is now a TV celebrity, thanks to a makeover and a talent for
reviewing pop fiction. She's at the top of her game—until bad boy author
Nick Angel tests her skills both as a reviewer…and as a woman.

### #419 AT HER PLEASURE  Cindi Myers
Who knew science could be so…sensual? For researcher Ian Marshall his
summer of solitude on an uninhabited desert island becomes much more
interesting with the arrival of Nicole Howard. And when she offers a no-
strings-attached affair, how can he resist?

### #420 SEX & THE SINGLE SEAL  Jamie Sobrato
*Forbidden Fantasies*
When something feels this taboo, it has to be right. That's how Lieutenant
Commander Kyle Thomas explains her against-the-rules lust for her
subordinate Drew MacLeod. So when she finally gets the chance to seduce
him, nothing will stand in her way.

### #421 LIVE AND YEARN  Kelley St. John
*The Sexth Sense, Bk. 6*
When Charles Roussel runs into former flame Nanette Vicknair, he knows
she's still mad at his betrayal years ago. But before he can explain, he's cast
adrift in a nether world, neither alive nor dead. Except, that is, in her bed every
night. There he proves to her that he's truly the man of her dreams!

### #422 OVERNIGHT SENSATION  Karen Foley
Actress Ivy James has just hit the big time. She's earned the lead role in a
blockbuster movie based on the true-to-life sexual experiences of war hero
Garrett Stokes, and her costar is one of Hollywood's biggest and brightest
actors. The problem? The only one she wants to share a bed with—on-screen
and off—is Garrett himself!

HBCNM0808